GEEK TO CHIC
Shirley Marks

When Silicon Valley engineer Nicholas Atwood donates two years' salary to charity, he is unwillingly thrust into the limelight. Aware of his social awkwardness and terrified of publicly disgracing his upper crust family, he seeks the help of a highly recommended image consultant. Maybe she can turn him into the perfect son, ideal brother, and articulate, gregarious foundation spokesman.

Doctor Kate O'Connor has transformed dozens of nerds into self-confident, socially successful men. Her foolproof method takes months, sometimes even years to work its magic, but Nick has just one week. Kate knows she's accepting the biggest challenge of her career to take on a project of this magnitude on such short notice, but as she helps uncover Nick's inner-hunk, can she handle the challenge to her heart when her feelings for him turn personal?

GEEK TO CHIC

•

Shirley Marks

AVALON BOOKS
NEW YORK

Published by Thomas Bouregy & Co., Inc.
160 Madison Avenue, New York, NY 10016

Library of Congress Cataloging-in-Publication Data

Marks, Shirley.
    Geek to chic / Shirley Marks.
        p. cm.
    ISBN 0-8034-9795-4 (acid-free paper)
    1. Engineers—Fiction.   2. Behavior modification—Fiction.
  3. Women psychologists—Fiction.   I. Title.

    PS3613.A7655G44 2006
    813'.6—dc22

                                        2006008518

PRINTED IN THE UNITED STATES OF AMERICA
ON ACID-FREE PAPER
BY HADDON CRAFTSMEN, BLOOMSBURG, PENNSYLVANIA

This story is one of transformation. It was inspired and shaped by those around me.

To Terry, Terry, and Rick for showing me that nerdy engineers are more than glasses, computers, and pocket protectors.

To my husband and best friend, for your love, encouragement, and amazing sense of humor. I can never thank you enough because you transformed me.

Chapter One

"One week? Impossible." Kate O'Connor had never heard of anything so crazy in her life. She glared across the table at her ex-client and one of many successes. She owed Daniel Latham because he'd given her business a great start, but what he asked just couldn't be done. "There's no way, just no way."

"Come on, Doctor O. you've got to help Nicholas."

"Is that why you asked me here?" A triple chocolate silk mousse served in an exquisite crystal dish, soft lights, and gentle jazz music did not make her more receptive to hard-luck cases. "Sorry. I'm not a magician. I don't have a wand to make it happen overnight, or even in a week. You'll have to tell Nicholas he's out of luck."

"He's not just another guy. He's one of my best friends. We've worked together for years, he's been my friend forever, and he really needs your help. I'm talking desperate here."

"Desperate, huh?" Ignoring the clink of utensils against china and the hum of conversation around her, Kate glanced around the subtly lit lounge to see if she could spot Nicholas. She had worked with nerdy engineers for so long that she could sense one in the same room.

A man dressed in baggy jeans and a T-shirt and sporting a short beard, ponytail, and square wire-framed glasses entered the room, heading for the bar.

"Excuse me," he said. His words were barely audible to Kate, but his outward appearance screamed *nerd*. "Excuse me." He held his hand up to a passing waitress who looked through him as she would a spotless window. "May I order a diet cola?"

"Is he wearing sandals?" Kate fought the urge to shake her head.

"A lot of software engineers wear that kind of shoe." Daniel sounded apologetic.

"The obvious course of action," Nicholas said to himself, "would be to sit at the bar where one would be able to place a drink order with the barkeeper."

Nicholas took his place on a barstool where he was ignored for more minutes than Kate wanted to count before he was noticed and finally ordered.

"He needs your help." Daniel was not going to give up.

Kate could see that.

Nerd didn't even begin to describe the guy staring at a glass of dark liquid on the counter in front of him. He made no eye contact with anyone. He sat round-shouldered and oblivious to what was going on around him, looking as if he were analyzing lines of software code on a flat-panel monitor.

But it wasn't his fault. He was being himself, and there was nothing wrong with that.

Everyone deserved love and acceptance, even unsociable engineers. Along with her PhD in sociology and her uncanny knack for straightening out the unsociable came a very successful business, but Kate had her limits. Her gut feeling told her that this guy was Mission: Impossible.

"I know what you're thinking." Daniel pointed his finger at her.

She sat back and smiled. A guy who knew what she was thinking would be a first. Men did not read minds.

"You know you can do it. I know you can do it. You can help him. You just don't want to."

Kate slid out of the booth before Daniel could stop her. But he moved quickly and had gotten to his feet by the time she made it to hers.

"You've helped every guy I've sent to you, and you've helped the guys they've sent." His eyes softened, and it hurt Kate to think she was letting him down. "Nicholas is not a lost cause."

Lost cause . . . that was a perfect description of the disaster sitting at the bar. "I don't necessarily think he's a lost cause. You know that the transformation takes months, even up to a year. The quickest change I've seen took six months, *months,* not weeks."

"Maybe you could give him some pointers."

Kate patted Daniel's arm and gave him a sympathetic smile. A few helpful hints weren't going to make a difference. She wished she could help. She might have tried if there were more time. But a week . . .

"I'm sorry, Daniel, really I am. I'm good, but your friend Nicholas needs a miracle."

At work the next morning, Kate's phone buzzed, and she hit the speaker button. "Yes?"

"Doctor O'Connor." Raymond's voice sounded a little odd, strained. Experience told Kate something was going on. "There's a . . . *gentleman* here to see you."

Kate glanced at today's schedule, which showed the next two hours clear.

"He doesn't have an appointment, but he's insistent."

"Can you make him one and have him come back later?" Kate suggested.

"He'd rather see you now," Raymond whispered, "and I don't think there's any time to waste with him, if you know what I mean."

"Why?"

"He's nothing like we've seen here before."

Kate could just see Raymond glancing over his shoulder nonchalantly for a peek. She had that haunting feeling the man in her outer office was Daniel's friend from last night. "Let me guess. Short, dark beard and straight brown hair in a ponytail?"

"Yeah."

"He's wearing thick glasses, a T-shirt, and those open-toed sandals?"

"Were you expecting him?"

"No." Kate eased down into her chair. "But send him in anyway."

Moments later, her office door swung open and Nicholas stepped inside. Kate already knew she would be turning him away. She had to hand it to him, though. Showing up in person took real guts. He didn't want to take no for an answer, but he would have to. It was the only answer that Kate was going to give.

"It's Nicholas, right?"

"That's right." Nicholas glanced at the wall that held her MA and PhD diplomas.

Kate smiled and gestured for him to take the chair

on the other side of her desk. "Please have a seat." On closer inspection, she felt certain that he was more of a full-year project than a short few months.

"I know this must be unusual but—thank you for seeing me so promptly, Doctor O'Connor." He sat, resting his hands on his thighs, and made no eye contact.

She crossed her legs and leaned back in her chair. "As I told Daniel last night—"

"Daniel approached you as my advocate, but I do not believe he can truly convey the urgency of my predicament." Nicholas' shaky voice sounded on the edge of desperation.

"He mentioned that you were looking for help." Kate wasn't going to say yes, not even maybe. But she didn't want to be rude and boot him out of her office. "And why do you need to be finished with the program in a week?"

"I thought if I could perhaps meet with you and explain. I am the guest of honor at a charity fundraising dinner, and I have to be *different*."

Kate knew what he meant by *different*: like a regular person, more normal-looking with more normal behavior. He didn't want to stick out, he wanted to blend in. Kate didn't have to know the particulars of why. It couldn't be done.

"I don't think the program will work by then. It takes nearly a year for most of my clients."

"Is there an accelerated course? I'm an excellent student." He glanced up at her, making brief eye contact. "I have full confidence that I can learn anything in an amazingly short span of time."

"I really don't think it's possible." Kate had seen anxious clients before, but that didn't necessarily make them better students.

She admired his determination. He *wanted* this to happen, and he was going to make it happen. But his transformation would have to happen without her help.

Nicholas leaned forward in his seat. "I'm willing to double your fee."

Kate shook her head. She wasn't going to do it no matter how much money he offered.

"T-triple." His breath caught, and Kate thought he might hyperventilate. "I may be donating my future salary, but I can assure you, I am far from without funds."

She looked hard at him. This guy was serious. It didn't matter, all the money in the world couldn't *make* her change him. And sometimes, no matter how bad they want to change, it just didn't work.

"It's not the money. The method is not a matter of teaching or changing you as much as it is a matter of self-discovery. I don't make engineer-to-man clones. I coax the inner man out. It's not an easy process, and there aren't any shortcuts."

"There must a way to achieve the same result. Please." Again his gaze met hers, and she saw how much this meant to him. "You must make the attempt."

"May I ask why this is so important to you?" She just couldn't imagine. He must have been nearly thirty years old. Why did he want to change now?

"I have to do this for my family, my mother and my sister. If I embarrass myself in public, I embarrass them."

The I-want-to-be-accepted look shone in his eyes. Kate knew the feeling, she was the one who didn't measure up in her family.

If he could come across as *normal,* they would see him differently, maybe even accept him. Love him? The more Kate looked at him, the more she couldn't ignore what he felt, and the more she wanted to help.

Nicholas shifted in his chair, looking more uncomfortable than he already was, if that were possible. "Seven months ago I made a substantial donation to the American Rainy Day Fund."

"Isn't that the foundation that provides financial aid to families impacted by natural disasters? Earthquakes, floods, fires, tornadoes, hurricanes?"

"Exactly. I returned to California a week before last year's Gulf Coast flood. There were forty-seven employees at that office. There were five on my team. Carl Kelly was the only one left. The others . . ." He cleared his throat. "I, of course, realize that they aren't the only ones affected. I felt the need to help. I haven't any medical or carpentry skills to contribute, but I can provide funds to hire the people they most need.

"I did not make the donation with the idea of impressing anyone. I was to remain anonymous. However, somehow I did not remain so. There are others in the company who are making sizable gifts, and our company is matching employee contributions dollar for dollar. In turn, other Silicon Valley companies are urging their employees to take action and— let me just say that I have been given the undeserved credit."

He was being modest. "That's quite an accomplishment. You've managed to inspire the whole valley," said Kate.

"Subsequently, the city discovered my role and Billy Barton decided he wanted to reward me with a party celebrating my success."

"The mayor?"

Nicholas flashed a nervous smile. "I declined, of course. I did not want to call any attention to myself."

Kate didn't blame him. Although she could see he was serious in helping the cause and encouraging others to do the same, Nicholas came across as introverted. The limelight wasn't what he wanted.

"Just as I was about to decline the honor, Mister Barton altered the event into a charity fund-raiser.

This would mean more money for the foundation's families, the children. I could not refuse."

"No, you couldn't." Kate could sense his anxiety. He felt trapped. On one hand, he wanted to be there to help, on the other, he risked hurting the family he loved.

"I've never been the favorite." He looked down at his hands, folded in his lap. "My sister is terrified that I might disgrace the family name."

Kate didn't know what to say. She knew exactly what he was going through, because it had happened to her. She was the one in her family who was ignored, passed over in favor of her brothers. She wasn't important. She was a girl.

Her parents didn't expect her to go to college or have a career. They expected her to marry, settle down, and raise children. But that wasn't what Kate wanted.

She knew Mr. Right was a myth. Kate had always wanted to help people. She had found her niche with helping slightly antisocial men find the gregarious man inside.

And if there was anyone in need of her help, it was the man who sat before her. How could she turn him away?

She couldn't say no to him, not now, not after knowing his reasons for wanting to change. If she were Nicholas and she had a chance to win her family's affection, wouldn't she do it?

If he were willing to try, why shouldn't she?

"When can we start?" There wasn't a minute to waste; Kate had just one week, and she wasn't sure how many hours of each day she could work with him.

"Officially, I'm still at work, putting in forty-plus hours a week." He paused. "Or whatever time it takes to accomplish my goals."

"And unofficially?"

"Per my employer, I am to take as much time as I need to resolve this issue."

Issue. That was a different way of putting it.

"We'll start immediately."

"Now?" Nicholas choked, sounding shocked.

Her sudden change of mind must have taken him by surprise. Or had he so little confidence that he would be able to convince her to drop everything and start working with him this very instant?

She lifted the phone receiver. "Raymond, we're going to need a car for the afternoon."

"Right away," her assistant replied.

"First things first." Kate pulled a folder from her desk drawer and handed it to Nicholas. "If you would fill these out. The contract is first; under it is a personal information packet."

"I can't tell you how much I appreciate this." Nicholas flipped thought the papers, eyeing each one. "Thank you very much for helping me, Doctor O'Connor."

Kate smiled. "You want to change. The least I can do is try my best to help."

Raymond stepped into her office while Nicholas filled out the forms.

"The car should be here within the hour," Raymond whispered to Kate.

"Good. Clear my schedule for the next week. Reschedule everyone."

"Done." Raymond noted it down.

"I want you to give Mikko at Clip and Michael Harding at Manfred's Men the heads up. I want to see them the moment we get there. Make appointments for a polish and the PT for tomorrow. Have Ben work up a daily schedule for Nicholas. Oh, yes, and make sure we see Doctor Keenan by the end of today."

"Got it." Raymond stared at his PDA, tapping the stylus on the screen and nodding at every instruction, and left to make it all happen.

"Doctor O'Connor." Nicholas handed the forms back to Kate.

She settled behind her desk and skimmed over his answers on the questionnaire before speaking.

"Your transformation will start on the outside."

Kate narrowed her eyes, looking at him carefully, trying to see how much of this was sinking in.

"The exterior changes, wearing new clothes and having a new hairstyle, will make you *look* different. Sometimes, most of the time, it makes you *feel* different. We'll build on that small change and add to it minor behavior modifications. Little by little, perceptions of those around you alter, and when others interact with you differently, you begin to change."

"Are you quite certain all this can happen in seven days?" Was that a hint of uncertainty in his voice?

"That's why I have doubts that this will work, but like I said, we can try. Inside is always the most difficult. You have to think about how you conduct yourself, mannerisms, behavior, and how others perceive you. This will not be easy. I need you to promise me that you'll do whatever it takes."

Had he realized what he was getting into? Kate watched him, studied him, looking for a reaction. *He had nice eyes.* Even hidden behind the large-framed glasses and his curtain of nerdiness, Nicholas couldn't hide his best feature.

"I'm ready to proceed." Nicholas straightened, looking determined. "And I am ready to do, as you say, whatever it takes."

"Good. I'm going to videotape this session, if you don't mind. We'll use it later for comparison.

Most men don't believe they've changed as much as they have."

Nicholas glanced around; Kate guessed he was looking for the camera. She opened her desk drawer and hit the record button.

"We'll start with your name. Once we have a new name to attach to your new persona, it makes breaking old habits and forming new ones a bit easier."

He nodded.

"Nicholas is the name you associate with yourself, the man you are now. Other people use that name, and that's how they think about you—as Nicholas."

He looked confused. As brilliant as they all were, the new clients always had a hard time grasping the concept.

"What if we shortened it to Nick?" It sounded good to Kate. "Nick is a nice, strong-sounding name."

"As in accidentally clipping one's self with a sharp object?" Okay, so he had some doubts.

She liked it, and the more Kate thought of it, the more she thought it suited him. "I think you need to get used to it."

"If you say so." He gave in.

"Any time you're ready, Doctor O'Connor," Raymond's voice interrupted over the intercom.

Kate acknowledged Raymond and asked him to tell the driver to stand by. She skimmed the rest of the first page of Nicholas's information.

"You've written here that you live with . . . with your . . . mother?" Grown men living with their mothers went out with . . . with the Macarena.

"I have Carl Kelly and his family living in my house at present. He has a wife and two kids. I've found it simple enough to return to my childhood home."

"But isn't she the reason you're here in the first place?" Living with her wouldn't help Nick's cause.

"My mother *and* my sister."

Nicholas couldn't go back there, because he needed to grow and learn to be his own person, a new identity. He needed encouragement and support, something that Kate doubted he would receive from his mother.

"I don't think it'd be a good idea for you to live with her while you're trying to change yourself. Something tells me she wouldn't be too supportive." Kate could almost see the gears in his head turning as he considered her words.

"What you say has some merit."

"Is there somewhere else you could stay for a while . . . ?" Kate stopped. "Wait a minute." Sometimes she was brilliant. "Daniel." She hit the intercom button. "Raymond, get Daniel Latham on the phone." She looked up at Nicholas. "He's the one who referred you. I'm sure he'll be more than supportive. As a matter of fact—"

"Doctor O., Daniel's on line two," Raymond said over the intercom.

Kate hit the speaker button. "Hello, Daniel."

"Doctor O'Connor, what's up?" Daniel's voice filled the room. With a couple punches of a button, Kate lowered the volume.

"We have a bit of a problem here, and I thought you might be the perfect person to help us."

"Who's *we*?" He sounded cautious.

"Nicholas. He needs a place to stay while he's going through the program."

"What? You're helping him? That's great, Doctor O. I knew you wouldn't let him down."

Kate had decided to help Nicholas, whether or not she had let him down was yet to be determined.

"No problem, he can stay with me." There was silence on his side of the line for a couple of seconds. "He's the best, Doctor O. Really. You'll never meet another guy like him."

"I don't w-want to impose on your privacy, Daniel." Nicholas leaned forward in his chair to speak.

"What privacy? No problem. I'm glad to help out."

"You've already completed the program," said Kate. "You know exactly what he'll be going through. You'd be a great roomie for him." She couldn't imagine a better situation.

"Swing by whenever and pick up the key." Daniel sounded happy for his friend.

"He'll be starting some intensive work the moment we hang up." Kate stared pointedly at her new student. She meant it: they had no time to waste. "I don't think you'll see him until very late tonight."

"I should be home from work after nine, probably hit the sack 'round midnight. If you get there after that, I'll leave the side door unlocked so you can get in. I'll put an extra key on the table by the front door."

"Thank you, Daniel. You have my gratitude." The ends of Nicholas' mouth twitched up into a shy smile.

"Any time. It's the least I can do for you."

"Thanks for giving us a hand." Kate moved back around her desk. "We'll be talking to you later, then."

"Sounds good. Good luck, buddy. Work hard. 'Bye." The line clicked as it disconnected.

"That worked out well." Kate turned the video recorder off and picked up her purse.

"Should I go home and pack a few things I might need?"

"There's nothing there you'll need. *Nick* is getting a new everything." Kate walked to her office door and motioned for Nicholas to follow.

"Come on, our ride is waiting. You can call your mother from the car. Tell her you're not coming home and that you'll see her at the Rainy Day fund-raiser."

Chapter Two

At 10:17 AM, the town car dropped Kate and Nicholas off at Clip. Raymond continued on to Manfred's Men to prepare for step two of the Nicholas-to-Nick makeover.

Clip was an upscale hair salon, and Mikko looked more avant garde than he was, but he did know hair.

Mikko wore his straight jet-black Asian hair parted in the middle, swinging just above his shoulders, framing his face. Kate wasn't sure whether his ultrathin glasses were necessary or just fashion.

In any case, the black of his hair matched his frames, shirt, slacks, and shoes. The fuchsia plastic body apron provided the only contrast and gave him a trendy appearance.

"*Number one,* get rid of the beard," Mikko decreed.

Nicholas' eyes widened.

"Remember, you said 'whatever it takes,'" Kate reminded him. When she said *changes,* she meant any and all necessary.

Nicholas took a deep breath and with a curt nod accepted his fate. He nearly shot out of his chair when the buzz from the clippers started, and leaned away when Mikko approached his face.

"Wait—please," Nicholas pleaded, holding Mikko's arm at bay. "If you would—" His gaze darted to Kate. "Allow me, please. Allow me to remove my own beard."

"You'll shave it off?" Kate imagined that maybe in this case all the changes didn't have to happen immediately. "You promise?"

"Tonight. I'll shave it off tonight. I promise."

The buzzing sound ended, and the clippers were gone. Mikko raised Nicholas' ponytail with a forefinger and an unpleasant look on his face like he'd taken a bite of bad sashimi and declared, "*Number two,* this comes off."

With one quick, efficient snip of the scissors, the ponytail was gone. Nicholas had no time to object.

Mikko swung Nicholas upright in his chair after washing his hair. Nicholas squinted, wrinkling his nose, trying to focus on his image in the mirror.

"You want a classic, sophisticated style?" Mikko shrugged. "No time—too many hours in front of the mirror. A short, spiky style?" He glanced at Kate. "Need too many products, too much time."

"He's a clean slate," Kate replied. "What would you recommend?"

Mikko combed Nicholas' wet hair this way and that, testing where it wanted to lie. Kate had seen him do this plenty of times.

"What do you think?" he asked Nicholas.

Nicholas gave a small shrug from under his plastic cover.

"You've worn a ponytail so long, you need something easy." He stared at Nicholas in the mirror.

"Good idea," Kate answered for him.

Nicholas just squinted, saying nothing. Kate hoped his face wouldn't wrinkle permanently.

"You're a pretty man. Anything would look nice."

Great. Kate had herself a *pretty* man, whatever that meant. Mikko had never said anything like that before about one of her clients.

"I think a nice, natural, messy look for you. Nothing fancy. All you need is a good cut." Mikko combed up a strand of hair straight from Nicholas' head, held it between his fingers, and sliced through it with his scissors.

"I can see *Nick* emerging," Raymond said about the new haircut when he met up with Nicholas and Kate at Manfred's shortly after eleven. "But the porcupine face doesn't fit," he added, wrinkling his nose and smoothing his well-tailored vest with both hands.

"I've given my word to shave the beard off tonight." Nicholas brushed at the neck of his T-shirt.

"He'll need a fully-stocked shaving kit by the time we get back to the office," Kate added to the ongoing list of instructions to her faithful assistant.

"Purchased," Raymond answered with another couple taps of his stylus on his PDA.

Kate already could see a major difference with just the haircut. Nicholas' round head looked less severe replaced by Nick's new softly-layered style. She couldn't wait to see Nicholas without his beard.

"Doctor O'Connor, a pleasure, as always." Michael gave a shallow, polite bow. "And you must be Nick Atwood, very nice to meet you. I'm Michael Harding, your personal shopper at Manfred's Men." He shook Nicholas' hand, too.

Nicholas glanced nervously over at Kate.

"Michael will help us find a new look for you," she said.

"What do you want to accomplish today, Dr. O'-Connor?" Michael asked, ready to get to work.

"We want different, different, different. Socks to ties, overcoats to underwear, casual to dressy."

"Excuse me, but I'm sure I don't need all that," Nicholas protested.

Kate ignored him. "Get rid of those sandals and

into a decent pair of lace-ups. I want to see those white socks replaced by multicolored Argyles, and if he walked in here wearing white cotton briefs, I want him walking out with baggy, striped boxers."

Nicholas glanced down, at the front of his pants.

Kate had to be careful not to laugh out loud. "Pull out your measuring tape, Michael, let's get started. Raymond, take this down."

Raymond tapped on his PDA and stood ready.

"You have to remember," she said to Nicholas. "You're not just wearing clothes. You're creating an image that you'll project to everyone."

Nicholas stood stock still while Michael applied his tape measure. Raymond took down the measurements from Michael and noted Kate's stream of ideas.

"Start with one single-breasted suit and a few blazers."

"Whatever would I do with a suit?" Nicholas complained. "I never, repeat, never wear one."

Kate turned to him. "Trust me, you'll need a suit." Back to Michael. "We'll start with one blue and one white button-down shirt, a couple of pairs of pants, and at least three ties; a pair of black leather shoes; and a black leather belt."

"A few minutes, please." Michael excused himself. "I'll be back with a selection for you."

"For daily wear," she continued, dictating to Raymond. "Let's go with a couple of pairs of jeans and some casual slacks. Because he wore a T-shirt in, he's leaving without one."

Nicholas brought his hand up to his chest in a show of modesty that made Kate smile.

"Stock up on a selection of polo shirts in various colors, and a pair of white athletic shoes and a pair of nice loafers should do." Kate stepped around Nick. "As for other accessories, you'll need a wallet. We'll keep it simple: black billfold to go with the shoes and belt."

"Got it," Raymond acknowledged.

Michael returned. "If you'll just follow me to the dressing rooms." He gestured to the left and led the way.

Kate started to follow, but Nicholas cleared his throat, attracting her attention.

"Excuse me. I'd rather have him—" he pointed at Raymond "—accompany me to the dressing room, if you don't mind."

Kate's jaw dropped. "Why?"

"He happens to be a man and you're not," Nick pointed out. "You are female."

Nice of him to notice.

"But you know that Ray is—" But Nicholas had already left, and Raymond gave her a big smile, wiggling his fingers, waving good-bye. He seemed thrilled to have been chosen to help Nicholas in the dressing room.

Gay is what Kate was going to say, but if it didn't bother Nicholas, it shouldn't bother her. But it did.

"I would never peek," she said to no one but herself. Kate headed over to the waiting area near the mirrors and settled into one of the leather chairs. She couldn't understand how Nicholas preferred dressing in front of a gay guy instead of a seasoned professional woman who had helped dozens of men find their personal style.

Nicholas was just a man. He didn't have anything she hadn't seen before.

"Bertoni," Raymond announced the first time Nicholas had emerged from the dressing room, "Rudolpho" the second time, and the third, "Zamora."

Without his glasses, Nicholas squinted into the mirror. He didn't seem to care one way or another for any of the designers. After the third try, Raymond and Michael proclaimed they had to look no further. The Zamora was the one.

While Michael chalked the suit for alterations, Kate's cell phone rang.

"Hello?" It was Randy Nash with another tragedy about to strike that would demand Kate's personal attention. She didn't think Nicholas and Raymond would miss her. It looked like they were making the final fashion decisions and getting along nicely.

She shouldn't make a habit of leaving Nicholas. Kate would have to turn her cell off and work somewhere other than her office. There would be too many interruptions. It was, after all, only for a week.

Her home? Daniel's? Both? This was something else she'd have to play by ear, but for now . . .

"Raymond, I have to go back to the office. Will you finish up here and take Nick to Dr. Keenan's?"

"Will do." Raymond's attention never diverted from Nicholas.

"Contacts. Daily, extended wear, whatever he wants—no colored lenses. He wears them out the door." Kate dropped her cell phone back in her purse. "Take good care of him, will you?"

"I won't leave his side." Raymond was in one of his moods. It must have been all he could do not to salute.

"And be *nice*," she warned. "I'll meet you back at the office."

Nearly four hours later, Kate saw the town car pull up at the curb. She heard Raymond chattering as he and Nicholas entered the office.

"Was that Randy Nash who just left?" Raymond asked.

"Yes. Another catastrophe diverted."

"Nick chose the Ralston camel-colored monk-straps, and he should have gone with the Medina brown wingtips." Raymond glanced back at Kate over his shoulder. "I did try to warn him."

"All right, let the fashion police go off duty. How did the rest of the day go?"

"Fine. It's just . . . well." Raymond glanced sky-ward and sighed. "There was a slight problem."

"What?" Kate couldn't wait to hear this.

"I hate to be the bearer of bad news," he said in his overly dramatic way.

"What?" Kate's mind raced, imagining the worst.

"I tried to explain, because . . ."

"What already?" Then it hit Kate. "He mixed de-signers, didn't he?"

Raymond buried his face in his hands.

Kate squeezed his shoulder to reassure him. "You're the only one who'll know. Trust me."

"I won't be the only one. It'll out there for *every-one* to see, on his sleeve, his collar, his feet, his whole body." He indicated each body part as he listed them.

"Nick will not posing for *Suave*, *Today's Togs*, or *Bay Area Buzz*. I think he'll be able to walk around town without doing too much damage to his reputa-tion."

"On the other hand—" Raymond tilted his head to

one side, taking a moment to choose his next words. "Everything looked so good on him—even though he tends to choose comfort over style. I'd kill for a trim waist like his."

Kate glanced at the tailored fit of her assistant's vest. Raymond was not fighting the battle of the bulge.

"Talking about *him*, where is Nick?" She leaned toward the window, trying to catch sight of him.

"He's tucking his new duds into his car. I gave him a map to your house, and he's to meet your there." Raymond continued his original thread. "I'm telling you, I think he really could go places if he wanted."

"I'm glad you think he'll rise above his fashion faux pas." It was already nearly five, and Kate felt drained and tired. She'd spent the last several hours working with Randy Nash, and she knew she'd be working with Nicholas well into the night. Her mind was beginning to wander.

"Doctor O-Con-nor?" Raymond said again, more insistently.

"I'm sorry." Where was Kate's mind wandering off to? "Was there anything else you needed to tell me?"

"Well, Michael had lunch sent in. We really didn't have time to enjoy it because we were on the job."

Kate wondered how any of this would pertain to her or Nick.

"I thought the pasta salad should have had a touch more vinegar." Raymond held his thumb and forefinger the tiniest bit apart, apparently indicating how much more vinegar should have been added.

At least they'd eaten. Kate had found a half-dozen Dough Boy donuts, jelly filled, not exactly what she would have liked for lunch, but she managed to down one with a cup of coffee and call that lunch.

"I didn't find it tangy enough for my taste"—he barely paused for a breath between words—"and I can't tell you how relieved I was when Nick expressed the very same sentiment. Oh, look, there he goes." He pointed out the window.

Kate caught sight of the blue car leaving the parking lot.

Kate parked her sports car in her garage, waving to Nicholas, who'd parked his blue two-door hybrid in front of her house.

"Got your shaving kit?" she asked as he entered the garage.

"Right here." He held the leather bag out for her to see and headed toward her.

It felt a little odd having a man she didn't know in her house, but he was a good friend of Daniel's. And Daniel said Nicholas could be trusted. Trusted? Kate might believe it on a professional level, but when it came to personal, she couldn't trust any man.

Kate hit the button to close the garage door and stood in the doorway to the house. Nicholas seemed

more interested in his new shoes than the new sur-
roundings.

"You can get to work on that beard, and I'll see to
dinner." She led Nicholas through the kitchen, past
the living room, and stopped in the hallway. "There's
a bathroom right there you can use."

Chapter Three

Nick Atwood wiped the excess shaving cream from his face and just stared into the mirror. The guy looking back wasn't the same one who stared at him this morning.

Standing in front of the sink without his glasses and clean shaven, he bore only a passing resemblance to his former self.

He wasn't sure which was the most significant change—his short haircut, his clear vision without the aid of glasses, or the shock of seeing the chin that had been hiding under his beard for nearly a decade.

Glancing over his shoulder, he checked to see if someone were standing behind him—perhaps the reflection wasn't his.

No one was there, only him.

Would he ever get used to seeing himself like this? The reflection was his. The new him—Nick.

Externally, he had changed one hundred percent. Inside, he was basically the same. He wished that he could just as easily change the rest of him. Logic told him that it wasn't going to be that easy.

As Doctor O'Connor had said, looks weren't everything, but his new exterior would make a big difference. The people who knew him would unquestionably look at him differently than they had before. *He* looked at himself differently. The people he didn't know, the people he would meet at the party, would certainly form a different impression than if they had met the old him.

She was right. He needed more time, but he didn't have the luxury. Doctor O'Connor had set all her other clients aside.

What about her personal life? Surely an attractive woman like Doctor O'Connor would have a personal life. A husband? A boyfriend?

Nick didn't want to intrude. A man or lack of one was none of his business. All he needed to concern himself with was that she was holding up her end of the job and made certain that he did his part. And he would do his part.

He had to go with the change, not fight it. To get what he wanted, he had to apply her advice no matter how much he wanted to fight against it. She could help him, and he was going to take full advantage of it.

He would wear the clothes that were picked out for him, and, as promised, he'd shaved off his beard. He would do his utmost to follow Doctor O'Connor's instructions to the letter, regardless of the doubts she had about the time limit: he would make sure that this was going to be a success. He'd make his family proud.

Nick wiped the sink with the hand towel, soaking up the stray water that might have splattered during the three times he'd had to lather up and shave, removing every last trace of his stubborn beard before pulling on his pale yellow sweater.

He packed up his shaving kit and took one last glance in the mirror before making his debut for the instructor.

"Would you care for some assistance?"

Kate turned to look at him and stared. He stood taller and straighter than she'd seen. He'd already felt a shot of confidence from his new exterior and liked the results. The new and improved posture said that.

She'd always had a pretty good idea what to expect. Her clients had always looked better but oh, my. . . . In all her years of work, in all the dozens of men she'd helped, she'd never seen this much of an improvement.

He cleaned up *very* good. He looked amazing.

He'd pushed the long sleeves of his sweater to his elbows, exposing his forearms, giving him more of a laid-back, casual air.

Kate swallowed. Why was his makeover any different? Why was she reacting so strongly to his change?

Nick's eyes weren't that green the last time she'd seen them. Kate fumed—she had specifically told Raymond no colored contacts. Maybe his brown hair framing his face and the soft, pale yellow of his loose-knit sweater really brought out their true color.

"Is there a problem?" Nick's side-to-side glances told her he was uncomfortable. "Something wrong?"

"What?"

"You're piercing stare is making me exceedingly uncomfortable."

"Oh, I'm sorry." Kate shook the clouds in her head away. What the heck had she been thinking? "I was just admiring your new look."

"Has it turned out as well as you'd expected?" He grinned, a little shy or self-conscious.

"Yes. Yes, it has." *Liking it* wouldn't be putting it mildly.

The grin broke into a smile. He had a great smile. Kate realized that she hadn't seen him smile before. It made her sad to think he'd never had a reason to do so until now. "How does it feel?"

"Different. Good different." He paused, then said something else before he glanced away. "You're staring again."

She *was* staring.

"I'm sorry." Kate couldn't help it. "Did you say something?"

"I thought you'd be preparing dinner, and I thought I might assist you."

"Preparing as in making dinner? Me?" Kate chuckled. "The only thing I *make* for dinner is reservations."

"I apologize. I never meant to imply—"

"That's all right. I called for a pizza." Kate had the strangest feeling of inadequacy. She didn't cook, and she'd never felt bad about it before. Why did it matter when she admitted it to him?

But there was something about Nick that made her feel—what? That she wished she could make him dinner? She never wanted to cook anything for anyone in her life.

Crazy.

Shake it off. She was getting some kind of nesting urge from him. It was like he triggered her well-buried domestication gene or something.

As if she *liked* him? Her? It was silly to think she'd be attracted to him. Attracted? She'd never been attracted to any of her clients. And she wasn't attracted to Nick—she couldn't be. It would take more than his straight, pearly whites to make her insides flutter.

She was nervous, that's all. Kate had never had a client come to her house, and it felt strange.

"Is there something wrong? You're still staring at me."

Kate moved around to the other side of the kitchen, putting the marble island between them. She had to be honest with him, tell him what she really thought. Isn't that why he'd come to her, for help? He had no social skills. He had no idea why she'd been gawking at him.

"You have a nice smile." Telling him made her feel peculiar, as if she might be telling him some hidden, secret feeling. It shouldn't have, it was her job.

"I do?"

"Yes. You should do it more often."

"Okay." He glanced down, embarrassed by her encouragement.

His bashfulness was sweet, adorable.

The doorbell rang.

"That would be the pizza delivery guy. I'll be right back." She headed for the front door and swung back to face him. "You want to grab some plates and a couple of sodas?"

Kate paid the pizza delivery guy and carried the medium pie back to the kitchen.

"You're not a vegetarian, are you?"

"No." He placed a knife and fork on a folded napkin by each of the plates at the kitchen table.

"Good. I didn't know what you liked, so I just got a combo."

"That's fine."

"Help yourself." Kate couldn't help but be fascinated by Nick's table manners. They were impeccable. He cut the slice of pizza with a knife and ate it with his fork, never once touching it.

This guy really needed to loosen up.

"You know, I've never taken on anyone who wanted to make the change so quickly. I think it might be a good idea, in your case, to take more drastic action."

Nick blotted his mouth with a napkin. "What do you mean by drastic?"

"I think since you only have about a week that we've got to make some major behavioral changes. Don't do anything that you normally do in the way you're used to doing it."

"Alter my routine."

"That's right." Engineers will be engineers, and some were more anal than others. How difficult it would be for Nick to change his routine would depend on how he rated on the anal scale. She just hoped he didn't peg the meter. "You want to change how you do everything. How does that sound?"

"Like I said, I'm willing to try anything."

"I want you to put down your utensils," Doctor O'Connor ordered.

"My . . ." Nick stared from the pizza on his fork that had only made it halfway to his mouth, to the knife in his right hand.

"Down. Put them both down now." She sat there, waiting, watching him.

He did. Nick left the uneaten piece of pizza on his fork, resting it on the edge of his plate, and set the knife parallel by its side.

"Pick up that slice of pizza and eat it."

"With my fingers?" Confusion set in. He wanted to, but he knew what he should do. His mother told him to never touch his food; one with manners always used utensils.

"Trust me," she insisted. "It'll be good for you."

Good for me? On the other hand, Nick had promised to do everything Doctor O'Connor told him or at least try. If she said to pick up the pizza and eat it, he was going to do it.

Nick lifted the slice, smiled, and took a bite. The roof overhead did not cave in on him, but Emily Post might be turning in her grave.

Direct contact with pizza left only a slight oily residue on his fingers. He could survive this. Nick took another bite.

"Another thing you need to think about is what you're saying. You need to relax, don't take things so literally. Your words and word choices need to be simplified."

"I'm not sure I understand."

"I'm generalizing but most engineers, when they speak, they're very precise. Most of the time it's too much information."

"Too much . . ." How could someone have too much information? Wouldn't someone want to know all the facts if they had bothered to ask you a question in the first place?

"Most people are on a need-to-know basis, you know?"

He nodded and said, "No."

"For instance, if your next-door neighbor Frank asks how you're doing, he really doesn't want to know *how* you're doing, not like your doctor who wants to hear about every ache and pain you have."

Nick wasn't sure what his neighbors had to do with what he was doing. "My next-door neighbor's name is Darryl on one side and Gary on the other, not Frank."

Doctor O'Connor's eyes lit up. "My point exactly."

"I beg your pardon."

"It's just an example; it really doesn't matter what your neighbors' names are."

"Oh." Just talking to talk never occurred to him before.

"If you're having a conversation, a social conversation, especially with someone you don't know, you want to lighten up on details of your information."

"Oh, so what you're saying is . . . less is more."

"No, it's just sometimes less is best. First impressions," Doctor O'Connor stated simply. "The very instant after someone sets eyes on you, they've formed an impression. So just the angle of your body in the way you sit, the stiffness in your body when you stand, makes a difference. That's the next thing we want to work on."

She wiped her hands, pushed away from the table, and pulled her chair to the center of the room, motioning him over to take a seat.

"I'm sorry but you're going to get awfully tired of sitting, standing, and walking. That's about all we're going to work on tonight."

"I don't find any of those tasks individually daunting," he said truthfully.

Doctor O'Connor gazed at him wide-eyed with eyebrows raised. Had he already forgotten what they'd just talked about?

"Did I say something wrong?" Nick's posture stiffened with every word.

"What did I just say about your word choices? *Individually daunting?*" she mimicked. "Okay. We're going to work on your posture." Doctor O'Connor took hold of his shoulders and moved them around, coaxing them to relax. "Now let your spine touch the back of the chair. Now do the opposite. Relax into the chair."

Nick let his shoulders sag and slouched back. "This isn't very comfortable."

"It's not supposed to be. We're just doing a little

exercise here." She tapped him on the shoulder, asking him to lean forward. "This time, let your spine just touch the back of the chair. Keep loose and don't let your body stiffen."

His shoulders didn't round, and he sat relaxed, just the way he should.

"Good." Doctor O'Connor stepped back. "You'll need to practice but that looks better. How does that feel?"

"Odd." He could hear the strangeness reflected in his voice.

"You'll get used to it. This is how you need to sit."

"From now on?" If just sitting was this hard for him, how would he learn everything else?

Doctor O'Connor took a step back, giving him room. "Now stand."

Nick stood and tried to do "relaxed" the best he could.

"Straighten up a bit." She ran her fingers up his spine and he felt every vertebra click into place. "You're so nice and tall with such broad shoulders. Let everyone see your handsome face."

Handsome? She thought he was handsome? Nick couldn't help but smile.

"That's it. Wonderful." She smiled back. "Why don't you walk across the room?"

He took a few awkward steps. He felt very self-conscious strolling across the room with someone watching every second. But it was *her* watching, and Nick didn't mind that so much.

"Again, try not to hold your body too stiff. Look strong, confident."

"Strong, confident," Nick whispered, hoping it would help cement the concept into his subconscious. "Not stiff." His back may not have been so straight and his shoulders not so broad, but he was working on it as he moved forward.

"Don't be hard on yourself," Doctor O'Connor said in a soothing manner. "It's difficult not to feel awkward. Just give it some time and keep trying. This is only the first day, the first few hours. I don't think there's any way you can pick this all up and have it feel natural."

"Of course, that only makes sense." He walked back and forth again.

Nick was conscious of the movement of every limb. Was he doing it right? This was something he would have to do without thinking. He felt his smile weaken then fade from his face. Maybe she'd been right—a week wasn't enough. The way he felt right now, there wasn't enough time in the world.

Chapter Four

Nick returned to Kate's house early the next morning. Kate pulled two mugs out of her cabinet. One was for her and the other for Nick.

What she was feeling last night . . . what she *thought* she was feeling—it was nothing. She had been tired, that was all. They'd been up too late, working too hard. Kate would have guessed that she wanted his transformation almost as much as he did. And he wasn't letting her down. He was working hard to understand what he was doing, to make changes.

Nick walked into the room and Kate did a double-take. Then she took a third look. He managed to dress himself fine, with Daniel's help, Kate guessed, but his hair . . .

"Hold it right there, Slick. Please don't tell me you

left the house looking like that." He'd combed his wet hair back flat against his head.

"Like what?" Nick looked down at himself.

She knew he'd never be able to find the problem—not without a mirror and not without a little fashion education.

"Am I wearing the wrong slacks? Daniel said—"

"No, your pants are fine. It's your hair." She paused. "Didn't anyone tell you that the *wet head is dead*?" He didn't get the joke, and he still hadn't a clue to what she was talking about.

"No one told me that." He seemed genuinely baffled.

"Let me pour you a cup of coffee before we start a new episode of *The Kitchen Beautician.*"

Nick swept his hand over his flattened hair, still looking puzzled.

Kate filled his cup and gestured toward the table. "Have a seat. I'll be right back." She handed him the mug and headed down the hall.

Kate snagged a hair dryer and a hand-held mirror, then returned to the kitchen.

"Here, hold this." She exchanged the mirror for his cup. "I take it you've never used a hair dryer before."

"No, I haven't." He stared at it like it was some kind of torturing device from another planet.

"What you want to do is add some body to your hair as you dry. So you have to lift it and—"

Nick held the mirror in front of him and watched, waited. Kate hesitated, not sure how to approach his head. The idea of touching him gave her goosebumps.

"Do you have a comb?"

Nick pulled a comb out of his back pocket and handed it to her over his shoulder.

She flipped the hair dryer on and ran the comb through his hair. It wasn't working well. What she needed to use was her fingers.

Touch him? His hair?

It seemed so . . . personal. Her goosebumps got goosebumps.

This was a new kind of "hands on" with a client.

Come on. She gave herself a mental shake. Nick was only a head of hair. Kate set the comb on the counter and used her fingers, pulling it straight for the moving air to dry.

"You want your hair to have the wind-tossed, casual look," she told him.

He had strong, thick hair. Just touching it make Kate go weak at the knees. She caught herself almost rubbing his head instead of drying his hair and told herself to get back to work.

But he had great hair, he had great eyes, and when he smiled at her . . .

Keep focused!

After several minutes, she had fluffed and dried

his hair, making it look almost as good as Mikko had yesterday.

"What do you think?"

Nick studied his reflection and flashed one of his killer smiles. "All that work for a *casual* look?"

"That's the secret, you have to make it seem like you didn't *do* anything at all." Kate unplugged the dryer.

"Sounds confusing."

"It is confusing. A lot to learn in a week, and today will be your first full day." Kate set her coffee cup in the kitchen sink and opened her briefcase on the counter.

Full day. Nick wasn't sure how he would last through a full day of instruction. Last night had been tough enough.

"We'll head into the office and—" She flipped her Daytimer open.

"The office, right now? What about breakfast?" He didn't know about her but he was starving.

Doctor O'Connor motioned to the coffee mugs and shrugged. Was that supposed to be breakfast? "And there'll be some donuts at the office."

Nick shook his head. A cup of coffee would not hold him until lunch. Not even a bowl of cereal would do. He needed protein, eggs, meat. Real food . . . *breakfast*.

It was one thing to change his old habits, but it

was another to starve. Omitting breakfast was not an option.

"I'll have to stop and get a bite to eat. What time do I need to be at your office?"

After consulting the day's schedule she said, "You have a meeting with your personal trainer at eleven."

"Personal trainer? Are you serious?" She was kidding, wasn't she?

Doctor O'Connor never cracked a smile as she did a quick check in her briefcase before picking up her purse and heading out the door. "Be at the office no later than ten, okay?"

He'd be there. Nick knew better than to argue about the personal trainer. If she said he was going to see one, then he would. It must be part of her "master plan." Working out wouldn't make a physical difference in a week's time, but it might make a mental one.

"I'll see you *before* ten."

"Cancel Nick's appointment with Doctor Campbell," Kate ordered on her way past Raymond on her way to her desk.

"Did you check?" Raymond at her over his right shoulder. "Is he cavity free?"

"You could say that." Kate couldn't imagine any tooth decay on any of Nick's pearly whites. His smile could grace a toothpaste commercial. "And get him a cell phone."

"He doesn't have a cell phone?" Raymond gave an exaggerated gasp of shock. "How can he live without a cell phone?"

"Says he never had a need for one. Until now." Nick still had to have a number his co-workers, family, and who-knows-who-else could call if they wanted to get a hold of him.

Raymond jotted it down on his PDA.

"We'll have time to work with him this afternoon. Last night we went over conversation and practiced walking, sitting, and standing. Maybe we'll go out for a test drive."

"You're taking him out?" By his reaction, Kate could tell that Raymond didn't think this was a good idea. "Already?"

"I've only got a week. We've got to keep things moving along."

By the time Nick sat face to plate with his Maddie's Diner's Magnificent Morning Meal, he didn't feel hungry. He flipped his bacon from side to side, making sure it was well cooked. Maybe he should have asked Doctor O'Connor to join him?

That was a strange thought. Why would she want to be seen in public with him?

Although he'd followed her suggestion of do-the-normal-things-different and ordered this instead of his stack of pancakes, he wasn't enjoying his breakfast as he normally had. It wasn't the bacon and eggs. He just wasn't in the mood.

He forked through his hash brown potatoes, which were usually his favorite, and couldn't help but think of her—Doctor O'Connor.

It was a good thing he was sitting when she styled his hair this morning. He might have gone weak at the knees and toppled over from the pure pleasure of feeling her fingers running over his head. Who would have thought something that negligible could feel so good?

What an impossible thought. Nick went to her for help, not a rent-a-girlfriend. He had to stay on track, keep his goal in front of him.

Nick stared at the plate of food and realized that this wasn't what he wanted. The sooner he got to work on himself, the sooner he'd change, and that's what he wanted.

He pushed away from the table and headed to the cashier to pay his bill.

What Doctor O'Connor thought about him wasn't important. Maybe a workout at the gym was what he needed. To be with other guys, get sweaty, and forget about women.

* * *

"Now don't be intimidated by Ben," Raymond warned Nick when they stepped into Big Ben's Gym. "He's all buff and no brains."

"Hey, Ray!" A guy, nearly as wide as he was tall, called out. Nick assumed this was the Ben person he'd heard so much about.

"This is Ben Meyer." Raymond gestured to him. "He'll be your personal trainer. Ben, this is Nick."

"Nice to meet you." Ben gripped Nick's hand so hard when he shook it that it was all Nick could do not to pry his hand away with his left hand.

It was like he had to prove something. He was bigger, stronger. Yeah, he was, but there was no need to pick on the weakling engineer.

"We got some work to do, right?" Ben clapped Nick on the shoulder, nearly knocking him over.

"I suppose so." Nick hated to think his physical welfare would be put into this man's hands.

"I'm heading back to the office," Raymond said to Nick. "I'll swing by to pick you up in a couple of hours."

Ben showed Nick the locker room and gave him a set of workout clothes, shoes—anything and everything he might need for this activity. After he'd changed into his gym outfit, Nick was taken from machine to machine, working different muscles. Ben never left his side. The actual *workout* didn't take much brainpower.

Nick noticed the women in the gym ogling and fawning over the muscle-bound owner. No woman ever looked at him like that. Then Nick wondered if women would look at him like that if he looked as beefy as Ben. And then he wondered if Doctor O'Connor would.

Giving one hundred and ten percent effort, Nick pushed for every rep, wishing, hoping the weight machine would make a difference.

"Your new phone." Kate handed Nick his ultra-trim cell phone when Raymond had brought him back to the office from the gym.

"Why do I need this?" Nick took the phone, and it was clear he wasn't sure what he should do with it. Who would ever call him?

"You're a man without an answering service," Raymond said with dramatic flare. "How is anyone going to get a hold of you? Your boss? Your co-workers? Your family? How about me—when I'm desperate to find you? I don't honestly know how you managed without one in the first place."

Raymond held up a Manfred's shopping bag between Kate and Nick. "And here are Nick's old clothes."

"Burn them," Kate prompted.

"Burn them?" Nick echoed, widening his eyes.

"We won't burn them, but you won't need them

anymore." Kate scooped up the bag handles before Nick had a chance. She opened the bottom drawer of her desk, dropped the bag in, and pushed it shut with her foot. "How was the gym?"

"Educational." She caught him squeezing his own bicep.

That wasn't an answer Kate would have expected to hear, but then again this was Nick. And Nick was no ordinary guy. "How so?"

"My initial impression was—"

Kate pinned him with raised eyebrows and one of those looks. One that told him he had to try harder to remember.

"Ah . . . I know. Let me try again." He took a few moments to find the right words. "It was my first visit. I had no idea what to expect."

"Good." She gave him the thumbs-up. "You didn't overdo it, did you?"

"No." His hand slid over his elbow to his forearm to give it a rub.

Kate thought she saw a hint of macho bravado coming from him. Couldn't be, not from Nick.

"Why don't we go over what you learned last night, and then you'll go out."

"Out?" Nick's staccato outburst didn't sound like it had come from him. "As in outside . . . with other people?"

Kate tried to hide her smile. Whatever male

hormone-induced high he might have had from the gym evaporated at the thought of interacting with total strangers.

"Don't worry, Nick. I'm not going to make you talk to anyone." Kate hid her smile and found his shyness cute. "Not yet. We just want to get you out with other people."

"Thank goodness." The sigh that came from him as he sank into the chair was priceless. As much as he wanted to overcome his shyness, he still held on to the fear.

Maybe he thought a full morning at the gym was enough. Something told Kate that Nick would be do fine, he could handle this. Not only would he surprise himself, but he might hold a surprise or two for her.

"Not yet, anyway. We have to save something new for tomorrow."

Chapter Five

Kate followed the Internet map directions Raymond had given her to Daniel Latham's house. Getting out of her car, she caught the most wonderful, mouth-watering scent of blended rosemary, basil, and garlic. It made her stomach growl. She glanced around, wondering whose dinner was cooking and what time she should show up at their house.

At the moment, food was high on her list of important things, but she and Nick had work to do. She'd just have to ignore her hunger pangs for now and worry about ordering takeout during a break.

Kate arranged to have Daniel meet Nick after he got off work. Maybe his friend's calming influence would have an effect, and perhaps anonymity would make a comforting combination during these first few days of forced public interaction.

Kate walked to the front door and rang the bell. The delicious aromas she had picked up outside were stronger. Were they coming from this house?

"Come in, it's open," Nick called out.

Kate let herself in and followed her nose toward the kitchen. Sounds of movement and metallic clanks grew louder. Kate rounded the corner to see three cooking pots sitting over flames on a gas stove. Nick stood at the counter with his back to her, busy chopping something.

"You're . . . you're. . . ." She pointed to the pots on the stove and knife in his hand.

"Cooking dinner," he finished for her, going back to his cutting board. "It's for us—"

"Dinner?"

"And Daniel, when he gets home. There's enough for him. I knew we'd be busy, so I thought I'd bake lasagna and freeze it for tomorrow's dinner. Maybe we'll take half to your house just in case we end up there some evening."

What the heck was he talking about? Just how much food had he made?

"There'll be enough leftover sauce for another pasta dish for later this week if we need it. And I have beef stroganoff simmering on the stove for tonight."

A buzzer went off and Nick leaped into action,

pulling a large pot off the stove and pouring its contents into the sink. Steam billowed into the air, and the scent of fresh pasta filled the kitchen.

Kate gave him a minute and let the steam clear. "Do you do this often?"

"Well, I . . ." He sounded semimodest about it all and didn't want to admit it when it was obvious that he knew his way around a kitchen. Even one that didn't belong to him.

She saw the realization hit him. He wasn't supposed to be doing what he usually did, in this case it meant cooking.

"Sorry. It never occurred to me. I thought if I took the time to prepare our meals in advanced we might . . . then we could have an early supper."

Kate set her purse on the kitchen table. "You're right, of course. But it's not in your best interest to do—"

"Things I'm accustomed to doing. Yes, I understand." He looked at the pots, pans, and dishes around him. "I must confess that I do not work well on an empty stomach . . . and I understand if you want to throw all this away."

"It would be wasteful." Kate admitted that the harm had already been done, but why throw out a perfectly good meal? Or two or three? She placed her hand over her rumbling stomach. "And it all smells so good." As if he couldn't see that by the drool that must have been dripping off her chin. She caught the aroma of the beef stroganoff simmering just off to her right. There was no way that was going anywhere except in her mouth.

"What if you helped?" he suggested.

"What?" Kate wasn't sure she'd heard right. "If I helped what?"

"I've never cooked with anyone before. I would be cooking, which is the same, but cooking with someone else is different for me."

Her? Cook? That wouldn't be different for her, it would be a first. Other than zapping a frozen dinner or boiling water for occasional instant oatmeal or freeze-dried noodles, she'd never really prepared a meal from scratch in her life.

"What can I do to help?" Kate guessed it would be a learning experience for the both of them.

"Let's see." Nick glanced around. "You can mix the salad for tonight while I assemble the lasagna. You'll find everything in the refrigerator."

Kate opened the fridge and stared at its contents. "Is it in a box? A bag? What am I looking for?"

"There's Romaine and Butter lettuce."

"Uh-huh." She grunted like she knew. *There was more than one kind of lettuce?* This was going to be hard.

"I thought you might be talking about one of those salad-in-a-bag deals."

"No, it's one of those head-of-lettuce deals. You break off the leaves, wash them, dry them, and tear them into a bowl."

Kate knew that. She'd seen salad made before. On TV.

"There's also some tomatoes, carrots, radishes, and celery that go in there. They need to be washed and cut up as well."

"I think I have my hands full with the lettuce." Kate pulled out two bags and headed to the sink, mumbling to herself, "Who died and made you king of cooks?"

"That's head chef," he corrected her.

Nick finished packaging the lasagna for freezing and made space at one end of the crowded kitchen table for them to eat dinner. They sat across from Daniel's stacks of mail and small boxes of on line purchases squeezed into one corner. Kate set the two bowls of salad in front of their cramped area and slid into her seat.

"Is there enough room?" Nick set a plate of beef stroganoff in front of her and one in the last empty spot, and squeezed onto his chair.

"Plenty," she answered just before she felt his calf brush against hers. "Oh, sorry." She pulled her legs back, tucking them under the chair. Kate mixed the sauce into the egg noodles and took a bite of stroganoff then froze, taking a little gasp of breath.

"What's wrong?" Nick seemed ready to leap into action. "Too hot? You don't like it?" He watched her and waited until she began to chew.

Kate swallowed. "This is delicious."

"Thank you." He shifted his legs before he started to eat, brushing his knee against hers. Their gazes met for an awkward moment. She speared a noodle with her fork and brought it to her mouth and licked a bit of sauce off her bottom lip, acutely aware that he had been watching the noodle's journey.

The feeling made Kate's mind numb and he might have apologized—or had it been a groan? She didn't know.

"There is something I'd like to ask." He stared at the lettuce in his salad and began to lay the leaves on one side of his bowl with his fork.

"Go ahead." Kate heard something in his voice change. She was curious to hear what was going on with him.

"The oddest thing happened to me when I was at the grocery store this afternoon."

"You went to the grocery store?" Kate was amazed that he had gone, voluntarily, to a place where there were people.

"That's where one goes to purchase food."

Kate wouldn't know.

"It was before I remembered that I should alter my routine. However, something different occurred."

"Tell me what happened." Kate twirled a bit of noodle on her fork.

"There was this woman . . . Sandy, who spoke to me." He began tentatively.

"What did *Sandy* say?" Kate felt a twinge of jealousy but dismissed it. Sandy had just as much right to shop in the grocery store as Nick had.

"She asked me if I wanted some artichokes."

"Artichokes?" That sounded innocent enough. "Maybe there was a special or artichoke promotion, and it was her job to tell shoppers." Kate didn't know the first thing about what went on in grocery stores.

"I don't think she worked there. She wasn't wearing the uniforms the other employees wore." Uncertainty filled his voice. "I told her I was interested in the broccoli and lettuce."

"And what did she say?" Kate's curiosity grew.

"She smiled and stepped closer to me to whisper, 'the milk was free.' I could see that she hadn't taken advantage of the free milk. I didn't see any in her cart. And in any case, it wasn't true. When I checked out, the cashier charged me the regular price."

Kate bit back a smile. Sandy had come on to him. Nick was getting hit on, and he hadn't a clue. This might have been the first time for him, but Kate would bet money it wouldn't be the last. He was in for a shock. Once he got out in the public, there wouldn't be a woman around who could resist him.

"Have you ever heard the saying, 'Why buy the cow if the milk is free?'"

"Of course I've heard of that." Nick instantly deciphered Sandy cryptic words. He cleared his throat and dug into this salad bowl with renewed vigor.

Kate gave him the once-over. For his own benefit, it was important that he know he had a natural charm, even a certain charisma. What woman would be able to resist his tall, well-built, broad-shouldered frame?

She watched the movement of his muscles across his strong, masculine jawline as he chewed. He glanced at her. A woman could feel her willpower wane once he focused his glorious eyes on her. And he'd seal the deal with that winning smile of his.

"I think . . ." Why was Kate having so much trouble telling him he was desirable to the opposite sex? She might have thought she was embarrassed saying it to him but that was silly. He had to know, and she had to tell him. It was her job. "Sandy struck up a conversation with you because she was interested in you. She found you attractive."

"Me?" Nick couldn't have looked any more shocked if Kate had told him he was sprouting a third eye on his forehead.

"You're a nice-looking man." Kate tucked her hair behind her ear, not a loose strand but a nervous gesture. "Very attractive, and some women are a bit more aggressive than others. She, Sandy, was interested in you."

Nick just nodded. Kate wasn't going to explain anything further unless he asked. There wasn't time to hold a debate on the pros and cons of being hot. There were things to be done, people to meet—

"I almost forgot. You're meeting Daniel at eight."

"I am?"

"You have to get used to going out and mingling."

"But I'm not ready yet."

"You're ready. You did it this afternoon and the more you do it, the more comfortable you'll feel." Did he think he could hide in the house until the fund-raiser? "You can only practice so much in an office or a living room. You don't have the luxury of waiting until you feel like it; you've got a party to go to."

Taking him into the outside world meant losing control. Sometimes it was exciting and sometimes scary.

"Sorry, Nick, I'm afraid it's time you face the real world."

Doctor O'Connor made Nick drive downtown and then left him in Daniel's care. Promising to return in an hour, she strolled down the street to find a bookstore. He and Daniel stepped into Global Coffee House and sat at a table in the middle of the room.

Nick had the worst feeling that everyone around him would know he was an imposter, being someone he wasn't. They knew, all of them, everyone. He was a phony.

They hadn't started making fun of him and laughing yet, but they would soon.

"No one knows better than I do what your insides are going through," Daniel tried to assure him.

Nick wasn't sure he was buying it. Then he remembered that Daniel, who before his own transformation was known as Danny, had gone through this exact situation.

"Your stomach is not only in knots, but you've got a whole battleship full of sailors tying them, right?"

Make that a whole fleet.

"The butterflies fluttering around are the size of the space shuttle."

Try butterflies the size of comets.

"And to top it off, you aren't sure if the Mount Vesuvius of stomach acid is going to erupt in front of everyone, making a bigger fool of yourself than you already feel."

That about summed it up.

The waitress brought them each a cappuccino and a chocolate-dipped biscotti.

"You've got to make yourself relax." Daniel took a sip from his cup.

"Yeah, thanks for the caffeine." It was easy

enough for Daniel to say. People weren't staring at *him*. Nick used his biscotti to stir his drink, trying to keep calm.

"Don't worry, it's decaf." Daniel continued. "Being out in public is the easiest thing. The people you have to be concerned with are the people who already know you. They're the ones who have a hard time changing to your change."

Nick hadn't thought of that.

"Take a look around. Go on." Daniel gestured with his cup.

Nick glanced from Daniel to a couple strolling by their table. There was a man standing at the counter by the entrance. There were several couples, sitting at tables throughout the bar, deep in quiet conversation. He watched a waitress cross the room behind them to the barista, standing by the cash register.

"All those people will accept you the way you are now. No questions asked. This is how they see you, how they'll remember you when they tell their friends they went out for a drink last night."

Thinking logically, Nick supposed Daniel was right. Who would take notice of him when they didn't know him at all?

No one.

Nick exhaled. He could finally relax. He hadn't thought of what he'd accomplished on his own. He'd managed to walk, say hello to the waitress, and take a seat without making anyone suspicious. No one backed up when they saw him or avoided speaking to him. There wasn't a single strange look directed his way. This was great.

"You're right. No one thinks I'm any different than the next guy." Nick toasted himself.

"That's right, pal." Daniel raised his cup and drank with Nick.

Bring on the fund-raiser. There wouldn't be anyone there he knew. No sweat. Everything was under control. All he had to do was avoid all the people he worked with and his entire family, and he would be okay.

For the rest of his life.

After saying good-night to Daniel, who took off for parts unknown, Kate and Nick stood outside in the cool evening air, waiting for the valet to return with the car.

Nick looked far more relaxed after meeting his friend. Kate wasn't sure what he'd said to Nick, but whatever it was seemed to have done some good.

"Atwood?" the car attendant called out.

Kate stepped forward and stood in front of the gleaming silver Bentley. "This isn't your car," she said to Nick who had been two steps behind her.

"Nicholas? Nicholas, is that you?"

Slowly, Nick turned away from Kate and toward the woman. "Mother?"

Mother? A well-dressed woman oozing class and sophistication gave Nick a once-over. The high-priced car belonged to that Atwood. *Mrs*. Atwood.

"Are you with this young woman?" she continued, now eyeing Kate.

Nick who appeared to be frozen to the spot where he stood wore a mixed expression of shock and dread.

"I'm sorry, this is hardly the place for proper introductions," Nick began, but his mother didn't look like she was going to move from that spot without them. "Mother, this is Miss Kate O'Connor. Kate, Mrs. Helena Armstrong-Atwood, my mother."

Helena Armstrong-Atwood turned her scrutinizing gaze on Kate. "Are you with Nicholas?"

"Yes, I am." Kate wasn't embarrassed to admit it. By the sound of Nick's mother, she should have been.

"How very nice to meet you." Helena's remark was followed by the smallest hint of a smile and a quizzical raise of her eyebrow. She turned her critical eye on her son. "I must say, I almost didn't recognize you."

How would she? Her little sonny-boy had changed into drop-dead handsome.

"Thank you," Nick replied, equally as cool. "But I can't take all the credit."

Mrs. Atwood turned to Kate. "I see that you've been a positive influence on Nicholas, Miss O'Connor." She glanced to her driver, standing by the open rear door of her Bentley. "I hate to do this to you at the last minute, but I'm having a tea tomorrow afternoon. Why don't you come, Nicholas? Both of you come."

Kate sensed Nick's hesitation and she jumped right in, answering for the both of them. "We'd love to."

"Splendid. Tomorrow, four in the afternoon, then." Helena Armstrong-Atwood gave a slow nod of her head and said, "It was nice to meet you, Miss O'Connor." She stepped into the back seat of her car, and the driver closed the door.

Once the car pulled away, Kate turned to Nick. "So that was your mother." Mrs. Atwood wasn't at all what Kate had expected. She seemed civil, cordial, with a layer of detached coolness running below the surface.

"Most people have trouble believing we're related. Especially her."

The two were vastly different, and Kate could well imagine that Nick, as adorable as Kate found him, might be a disappointment to his socially-minded, upper-crust mother. "Come on, you're too hard on yourself."

Thinking of Nick as an unloved child tore at Kate's heart. Knowing herself how much that hurt growing up, the look on Nick's face told her it was still going on.

Just because he hadn't turned out to be as debonair as his mother was sophisticated didn't make him a failure. Kate didn't know why she had the feeling that along with his newfound pride in impressing his mother, he harbored the fear that he might still disappoint her.

There was a lot of positive in Nick. Kate figured the real problem was that his mother hadn't bothered to take the time to get to know him.

Chapter Six

Nick had completely forgotten that his mother's favorite restaurant, Potage, was in the same building as Global Coffee House. What were the odds that they would bump into each other? The variables: the day, the time . . . He couldn't run the calculations off the top of his head, but he knew they were very, very slim.

"My mother can be difficult," Nick said once they'd gotten in his car and were on the way back to Daniel's house. He was certain attending his mother's tea was not a good idea. "I think we should call her and tell her we've changed our minds."

Kate didn't say a word, only shook her head slowly.

That nasty determined streak of Doctor O'Connor's made an appearance again. She wanted to go and he didn't, and he didn't know how to convince her otherwise. This wasn't going to be an easy battle to win.

He suggested that they could go out to somewhere else public, meet other strangers. Anybody but his mother's friends; he wasn't ready for that.

"Do I have to remind you that you have a fund-raiser in three days?"

No, she didn't.

"And at that fund-raiser you want to win the guests over, show them you're perfectly at home with public speaking and the media attention."

Nick understood, but there must be another way besides attending his mother's party. That might prove as stressful as attending the fund-raiser.

"Your behavior isn't going to change overnight, you know. You need as much practice, exposure as you can get."

"I know," Nick conceded and pulled up behind her car, in front of Daniel's house. Doctor O'Connor was not going to let up.

"You've made wonderful progress tonight with Daniel, and your mother's party is the perfect dress rehearsal for the fund-raiser. How about it?"

"You don't understand." How could she? He turned off the car and pulled out the key. Doctor O'Connor didn't know his mother. "My mother's friends are just as cultured as she is, as I'm not."

"But you're a local celebrity," she persisted.

"Most people will forgive a celebrity almost anything. There isn't a chance they won't like you. They'll want you to like them."

And from the way she said it, he believed her. In that situation, with him at the front of the room, the center of attention, with the mayor of San Francisco next to him, everyone would like him. He had to admit Doctor O. was right.

"You win," Nick conceded. "We'll go." If she thought this was the best was for him to hone his skills, he'd do it. Why did she always have to be right?

They got out of his car and slowly moved toward hers.

"Wonderful." Kate knew this was the perfect solution. "Do you know who'll be at the party?"

"Although I've never met them, I know most of them by name."

"Then meeting them for the first time will be a breeze, won't it?"

"Daniel told me that meeting strangers was the easiest of all. They don't have any expectations."

"He's right. And you're a great guy." That wasn't news to Kate. "And everyone at the party will see that, too."

"To admit that I've hired you . . ." Nick didn't want anyone to know about his anti-geek lessons.

Kate couldn't blame him for wanting to keep that a secret.

"We won't say anything about—" Kate motioned between the two of them, indicating what really went on between them "—this. We'll be just like any normal couple, okay?"

"You'd let my mother and all her friends believe we're *together*? But that's a lie."

Kate needed to convince him that telling a little white lie wasn't the same as lying outright. There was a difference, a subtle one, and it was something he'd have to learn: lying to be polite.

"I can't help what your mother believes. If she chooses to believe we're a couple, who am I to tell her she's wrong?"

"You don't mind, do you? I wouldn't like to put you in an uncomfortable situation."

"Don't worry, I think I can handle a little implied intimacy. And you're going to blow it if you don't stop calling me Doctor O'Connor. From now on it's Kate."

"Right, Kate." Nick closed his eyes as if concentrating to rewrite name protocols in his head. "Ka-ate."

He might have said *Kate* but it still sounded like *Doctor O'Connor.*

"It's getting late. We both need our rest." The hour was late, and to Kate, Nick looked more tired and stressed from thinking about tomorrow's tea party.

"You should be proud of yourself you've made great strides tonight. We'll get a good night's sleep and start fresh in the morning. How does that sound?"

"Anything you say, Doctor O'Conn-*Kate*."

The next morning, Kate walked into an empty outer office and noticed her door ajar. She glanced down the hallway, wondering if Raymond was getting coffee. Then she heard Nick's voice.

Kate peeked into her office and saw that Raymond had made himself comfortable in her chair and Nick was in the center of the room, balancing a book on his head while chanting, "The rain in Spain stays mainly on the plain."

Kate pushed the door open. "What do you think you're doing?"

Raymond stood and Nick stopped midphrase.

"Working," Raymond replied, caught red-handed like the rat he was.

"Ray-mond." Kate snatched the book off Nick's head, dropped it into her assistant's hands, and pushed him out the door. "Make sure we're not interrupted."

Raymond caught the door and leaned in to whisper, "You really have to work on his gullibility factor. Make a note: he'll believe anything and do anything you say."

"Out," she said more forcefully and pushed the door shut behind him. Kate knew she could mold

Nick like clay, but honestly there wasn't a single thing about him she wanted to change. She had to admit that she liked him as he was. "Sorry about that. Raymond sometimes gets too involved."

Nick sat on the sofa and looked uncomfortable.

"Are you worried about this afternoon?" Kate watched him carefully.

"I'm not nervous at all." But he couldn't look her in the eyes.

"If you want your mother to believe we're a couple, we're going to have to make some changes in the way we interact."

"What changes?"

"She might expect that we were close. Really close." The blank expression on his face told her he hadn't a clue to what she was talking about. "She might expect that we've been intimate."

"Oh." He blushed and cleared his throat.

Kate couldn't remember the last time she'd embarrassed a man. How about never.

"What—" Nick cleared his throat. "—exactly would tip off my mother that we hadn't been . . . you know."

"We both need to behave more . . . connected, like we've shared each other's company for a while."

Nick stared off, deep in thought. Kate wondered what he was thinking about.

"Couples usually stand closer to one another than

to other people. They touch." She laid her hand on his forearm, and he pulled his arm away, leaping away from her.

"That's exactly what's going to convince your mother that we're *not* together."

"You surprised me," he said, catching his breath. "You should warn me before you do something like that."

She didn't know why, but his flustering make her smile.

"And you can't jump every time I touch you." She laid her hand on his arm again. "I won't bite. I promise."

He returned her smile, but Nick's smile was tinged with nervousness. Would he ever relax?

"I didn't think you'd bite."

"You'll be all right. Just breathe."

Being paired up with her sounded too good to be true. It made him feel more nervous than meeting his mother's bridge club, fine arts league, and the Leland Ladies' Society combined. But one look at Kate and he felt his fears ebbing.

She stared at him with soft, wide eyes and her lips curved into a gentle, soft smile, melting his insides. He'd never felt like this before. Nick let himself imagine what it would be like if she looked at him like that for real.

I may even learn to enjoy it.

Kate. Kate. Nick loved her name. He loved hearing it, thinking it, and now finally saying it. Not just in his head but out loud.

"Don't forget you can't behave as if this weren't natural to us."

"Do you think it's possible? Do you think we can . . . we can . . ."

She stared from his eyes to his mouth and held. Nick couldn't catch his breath. He didn't know . . . didn't know . . . what was happening?

Kate leaned toward him. Her eyelids looked heavy, and she was losing the battle to keep them open. Moving closer, her smile faded.

Nearer, nearer.

His eyes closed just as their lips touched. The jarring buzz of the phone sounded, and they jumped back from each other.

"Doctor O'Connor, I have Randy Nash holding on line one for you."

"Excuse me," she swallowed and whispered to Nick. Kate moved over to her desk and picked up the receiver. "I thought I told you we were not to be disturbed," she scolded Raymond.

She paused as Raymond spoke.

"All right, all right. I'll talk to him." Although clearly irritated, Kate turned to Nick and flashed a small smile. "I'm sorry, will you excuse me for a few minutes?"

"Sure, no problem." Nick stood and left her alone in her office.

What did she think she was doing?

Kate was going to kiss him, *that's* what she thought she was doing. And pretending to be his girlfriend or not, she couldn't go that far. Holding hands was one thing, but kissing him was out of the question. That was a line Kate would not cross. That was getting way too personal.

But she wanted to. How she wanted to! Just the thought of him, only moments ago, leaning toward her, so close, ready to—

"Doctor O'Connor? Are you still there?" The desperation in Randy's voice was at its peak.

"Yes, I'm sorry. You were saying?" Kate refocused her attention on Randy's voice.

"I was saying that this is really a sticky situation. I know how I'm supposed to behave, but I'm really having a hard time conforming. Do you know what I mean?"

Yes, Kate knew exactly what he meant.

"You'd better have a seat," Raymond said to Nick. "This might take a while."

"Thanks, but I think I'll stand." Nick couldn't really stand, either. He paced to the front door and back to Kate's office door, he didn't know how many times.

They'd almost kissed. How could he pick up where they'd left off? He'd heard about 'being in the mood' and that was what he thought it might be. And how could he recreate the mood?

She was the one. Kate.

If he disgraced himself in front of her . . . He was caring less about what his mother's friends thought than Kate. He didn't want to let her down. He wanted her to be proud of him. He wanted her to like him.

"You're wearing out the new carpet," Raymond pointed out.

"What?" Nick looked over at Raymond.

"What's the problem? Is it this tea thing with your mother? Just keep your pinkie out when you sip." He demonstrated with an imaginary cup and saucer.

"No, it's not that. It's . . . all the other guests. What if I make a mistake? What if I say something I shouldn't? How will I know if I'm boring someone? It happens, you know. I bore a lot of people." And at times the converse: he didn't know when to shut up.

"Don't sweat the small stuff." Raymond gave a wave of dismissal. "Doctor O. will be right there, she won't let you get in over your head."

"But what if she can't help? What if she's across the room trapped by the local social columnist? What am I going to do?"

"She'll give you the thumbs-up"—Raymond demonstrated—"for a job well done, or a thumbs-down"—he reversed his gesture—"if it's a no-go."

"And what happens if I'm heading in the wrong direction, conversationally speaking? How will I know what to do?"

"Well . . . she can . . . well—" he paused and stared toward the ceiling until his eyes crossed. "She could always give you another signal."

"Signal? What kind of a signal might that be?" Nick stared, waiting to hear Raymond's wise words.

Raymond exhaled. "Anything that's prearranged, like, you know, the baseball players have." He went through a flurry of touching his head and tapping his shoulders with his hands, ending the routine with a slide of his index finger down his nose. "Like that."

"And what does all that mean?"

"That's the beauty of it." Raymond clapped Nick on the back, turning him toward Kate's office. "It can mean anything you want."

The door to Kate's office opened, and she watched them through narrowed eyes. "What's going on with you two?"

"I think I've just come up with a great idea," Raymond boasted.

"Have you?" Kate sounded skeptical, but as soon as he told her his idea she thought he was as much of a genius as Nick had.

"I didn't know you knew anything about baseball."

"I"—Raymond pressed his index finger to his chest—"am a fountain of information."

"I didn't think you were interested in sports. Doesn't matter," she shrugged. "It sounds like a good idea."

"This"—Raymond brushed his cheek with his fingertips—"for too much info, this"—he tapped his chin—"for shut your yap."

"I like it. How about if we practice some scenarios and see if there's any other signals we might need." Kate pulled her office door open wide and waved them in.

"Oh—and I have one you mustn't forget." Raymond tapped his chin with one fist, then the other.

"What does that mean?" Nick couldn't imagine.

"It means I love you," Raymond said in a sickening sweet tone and tilted his head for effect.

Kate glanced heavenward and pointed into her office. "Get in there before I fire you for real."

They spent a few hours of practicing conversational cues and came up with some new ones. Raymond's PDA alerted him that Kate and Nick had to leave for their next appointment.

"Far Oasis," he whispered to Kate.

"That's right." Kate rushed to retrieve her purse. "Come on, Nick, let's go."

"Go? Where are we going?" Nick stood and followed Kate out of the office door to the parking lot.

"We've got one thing to do before going to your mother's." Kate stopped, deciding which car they should take. She glanced over at Nick and decided, "I'd better drive."

"Where are we going?" he asked again while getting into her car.

"You'll see. It's not far." Kate pulled out of the parking lot and pulled into another parking lot six blocks away.

"What is this place?" Nick looked around, his growing suspicion clearly spreading across on his face. "It's not another salon, is it?"

"Not exactly." Kate pulled the door open and motioned for Nick to enter first.

"One stop before going to my mother's?" He checked his wristwatch. "Are you telling me this is going to take six hours?"

Nick spotted the business sign hanging in over the front desk: *Far Oasis Day Spa and Beauty*.

"What is this?" Nick asked warily.

"You're here for a treatment."

It was clear that Nick wasn't happy about this, nor had Kate expected him to be, but it's not like he had a choice, and he went along with the plan without protest.

Nick's treatment started with a scrub, then a facial

mask during his manicure and pedicure. A light lunch was provided, and the entire experience took almost three hours.

"That was weird." Nick squeezed his eyes closed and shivered when he got back in Kate's car. He inspected his nails and grimaced. "There is no way you're going to convince me that normal men have this done to them."

"Not all men, but some do. They don't call it a mani for nothing." Kate tried to take a peek at his nails while she started the car.

"Grapeseed rub with a honey glaze, avocado mask, and cucumber slices on my eyes, what's next? All they needed to do was add some lettuce and I would have been a salad."

Kate pulled out of the parking lot and turned on to the street. "You're supposed to be open-minded, remember? *Nick* is supposed to try new and different things."

"I have news for you. *I* didn't like it and I'm pretty sure *he* didn't, either."

"Don't be such a baby. It didn't hurt." Kate drove into her parking lot and pulled up next to Nick's car.

"It was stinky and gooey." He made an unhappy face recalling the whole thing. "And it was like an estrogen spa in there. Did you see all those women gawking?"

"They weren't gawking."

"They were gawking," he insisted.

"Oh, just get over it, already." Kate tried not to laugh and motioned him out of her car. "Before I go home to change, we need to do a wardrobe check on you. You head out, and I'll follow you home."

"What are you planning on wearing this afternoon?" Kate set her purse on Daniel's kitchen table.

"I thought the suit I thought I'd never have occasion to wear might be the way to go."

"You don't think the suit overdressing? Your mother said the tea was casual."

"A tux might be too much, but not a suit. I can assure you that *her* definition of casual is different from yours." Nick moved into the family room, sank into the sofa, and took another look at his neatly-trimmed nails. "I'm feeling nervous."

"You'll be fine. We'll be fine." Kate tried to reassure him. "You did a great job this afternoon. And you'll look fantastic."

She wasn't sure he was buying it.

"I'll look like a—"

Kate cleared her throat, trying to get back on track. "There is something else. We need to go over what's supposed to go on between us."

Nick's eyes widened, showing his interest. She had his total attention. He watched ever gesture, every expression she made, listened to every instruction, took to heart every suggestion she gave him. Kate had never held a man's attention so completely. And she found it very intoxicating.

"Just for added effect this afternoon, if you remember, while we're walking, sitting, or standing together, we might do it arm-in-arm or hand-in-hand—a close proximity, in any case."

"Like this?" Nick took Kate's hand in his and rested it on his knee.

The nervousness he'd had seemed to have disappeared. He seemed very comfortable with her touch—much more comfortable than she was touching him. She liked it too much.

"We can do this. It isn't so difficult." Nick sat closer, and she felt the warmth of his thigh against hers. "I think this is nice."

"It's supposed to be nice," she returned in a whisper and thought to herself how more than just-nice it was.

Thoughts of skipping the tea altogether and spending the afternoon lying in Nick's arms flooded her mind. Kate wanted to touch him, kiss him, tell him how wonderful she thought he was.

Nick moved closer to her, and she leaned in toward him. Kate could smell his clean scent, and alarm bells in her head rang, warning her she was getting too, too close.

The next thing she knew, Kate had slid her arms around his neck, holding him to her, kissing him. His chest felt firm and strong against her. His lips were eager but yielding, and his arms held her tight. He tasted warm and delicious with not a hint of the inexperience she thought he might harbor.

Kate's heart pounded, the blood rushing through her body, drowning out any common sense she might have had. She pulled away about two or maybe twenty seconds after she'd realized she was kissing him.

Yes, she liked it, but this was unprofessional no matter what she felt.

"Kate, I . . ."

"That should convince anyone who has any doubts." She stood, putting space between them. "I think we shouldn't think too much about this. I should get going. I've got to go home and get ready."

"Kate—" Nick tried again to say something.

Apologize? Say he liked it? Oh, she didn't want to hear that.

"Don't worry, all you have to do is be your charming, wonderful self. See you in about an hour, hour and a half?" She flashed him a smile, a nervous one. "Everything is going to be fine."

But Kate wasn't convinced everything was going to be fine. Sure, she could hide her feelings, and as for his feelings, because she knew there had to be some feelings on his side of that kiss, well . . . They didn't have time to worry about whatever he might have been feeling right now.

He—she—they would just have to deal with it later.

Chapter Seven

Nick wasn't sure how he ended up in his room. One minute he was sitting on the sofa, his arms wrapped around Kate, enjoying her warmth and softness, and the next he was here.

There was one coherent moment before their lips met. He caught a glimpse of Kate with her head tilted just to the right. Her eyes were closed, her lips barely parted, her whole face relaxed. When they'd kissed, he thought he'd died and gone to heaven.

He'd kissed a girl before, lots of times. He'd had two semi serious relationships. The first time was a teenage summertime romance. The second was in college, an awkward episode for the both of them. But a kiss had never felt like this before.

Kate's body had pressed against him, molded

against his. Her arms held him close, preventing him from moving away. Why would he want to? He could have stayed there forever.

Her hair smelled of warmth and softness. Her lips tasted of sugar and spice and everything nice. Nick wished he could remember how she felt in his arms, but his mind couldn't hold on to every detail. The memory fragments slipped out of reach as he tried to pull them together.

Sinking onto the bed, Nick drew in a deep breath and held it for a few seconds before letting it seep out. And the day wasn't over yet. Not only would he be with her for the rest of the day, he'd be half of a couple with her. As Kate had said, people would expect to see them together, behaving as though they were together.

He smiled to himself. Nick would be expected to hold her hand, touch her, and share her company. His mother's tea party was sounding better to him all the time.

He shaved and dressed, all the time thinking to himself about going the one step further for Kate. He wanted to impress her, he wanted her to be with him. She must have liked him; why would she have kissed him otherwise?

After a last check in the mirror, Nick straightened his new silk tie, ran a hand down each arm of his jacket, smoothing any wrinkles, and examined his slacks from the crease down the front to the tip of his polished Italian shoes. Nothing was out of place.

It was show time.

Nick stepped into Kate's house an hour later.

"Aren't you handsome, Mister Engineer." She eyed him, taking in every detail. If anything was out of place, Nick knew she'd be the one pointing it out.

"Your hair looks great."

"I put some stuff in it. Daniel gave me a 'product' demonstration." He fingered his hair out of nervousness.

Was he nervous? Forget his mother's friends, Kate made him nervous. He wanted to please her and hoped he would, more than anything else.

She could not have looked more beautiful. Her tea-length, soft floral-print dress was sleek and elegant.

"I still think you might be a tad overdressed, but there isn't a soul that can deny that you'll be the most handsome man there." She slid her hand down his lapel, smoothing it.

"You're as dressed up as I am." He motioned to her then to him. "There isn't any reason you should have to follow my lead."

"No matter what I think I should wear, since we're

a couple we should match, not matching outfits but in *dressiness*." Kate opened her purse and checked its contents.

"I never thought of that." She must know everything. Kate was smart in a way he could never imagine. The things she knew, etiquette, manners, social subtext. She was amazing, and Nick couldn't help but admire her.

"That's why I'm here." Kate tapped her shoulder. That meant *be nice and smile*.

"I get the message." Nick smiled. He'd memorized eight of them. All simple and, hopefully, helpful.

Kate stepped up to Nick and brushed the shoulders and lapels of his jacket.

"What does it mean when you brush my shoulder?"

"It means I want you to look nice." She stepped back and smiled, apparently pleased with his appearance. "Are you ready, Freddy?" She picked up her small handbag, slipped the strap over her shoulder, and headed for the door.

Nick glanced over to her and smiled. This was going to be fun. He couldn't wait. He liked the way he felt when he was with her and for the next few hours, he'd have Kate all to himself.

She caught his arm. "Are you sure you're okay with this? You're still not dreading the party, are you?"

He pulled the door open, waited for Kate to exit

first, and smiled. "I can't tell you how much I'm looking forward to this."

The drive from Kate's Los Altos house to Helena Armstrong-Atwood's residence in Atherton wasn't long. Atherton was where all the Bay Area's wealthy and local celebrities made their home. Modest tree-lined streets traversed the residential neighborhood. The lack of sidewalks and street lighting discouraged pedestrian traffic.

Tall, stately manors sat back from the front gates with driveways that wound back to the homes. Mature trees and massive plantings of bushes screened the street from view, and more important, any passerby's view of them.

Dark green shutters flanked two dozen double-hung windows on the front of the white clapboard siding of the Atwood colonial-style mansion.

"Don't worry. We're here to enjoy your mother's tea party just like everyone else." Kate blinked and smiled. "You'll be pleasant as always and polite as your mother has taught you."

"I hope it works." It should. Nick gave a reluctant nod of his head and opened the front door for her, allowing her to enter.

Their steps echoed in the marbled foyer on their way into the house. Voices came from farther back, past the front parlor and formal dining room, and

Kate followed Nick through the family room to where the guests congregated in the garden in the back of the house.

"I see what you mean by your mother's idea of casual," she whispered to Nick. "Oh, dear. They're all wearing hats." As well dressed as Kate was, her lack of a garden hat made her feel naked.

"I'm sorry, Kate. I should have remembered to tell you." Nick could not have sounded more remorseful.

A harp played in the background while they strolled between the large, dark green colored umbrellas which dotted the back yard, providing shade for the guests around the pool area just inside the lush gardens.

"Don't worry about it. I'm not here to impress anyone." But it did make her feel more like an outsider.

They continued toward the back of the yard beyond the pool, where a quartet played in the open-air pool house, providing background music.

Along the way, delicate china pots were displayed on crisp white linen tablecloths with a matching sugar and creamer set. A three-tiered plate rack held tidbits of fruit. Beautiful, mouthwatering biscuits sat on various tables.

Nick led Kate around the white wicker furniture and low tables that lined the patio. Every table had a centerpiece of roses, stocks, and hydrangeas.

"Nicholas, how nice to see you. I'm so glad you

both could come." Mrs. Atwood, under a wide-brimmed pink hat with light pink chiffon roses, pressed her cheek to her son's and bubbled with enthusiastic approval, eyeing him from side to side and head to toe. "What an exquisitely-cut suit. And you look so handsome."

Nick glanced at Kate, and she could tell he was about to say he'd had help with its selection. Kate touched her cheek, signaling for him to keep silent. He took Kate's advice and merely thanked his mother for the compliment, then allowed her to continue.

"Have you had a manicure?" Mrs. Atwood's gaze flicked over Nick's recently-tended cuticles and clear-polished, trimmed fingernails. "Amazing." She wasn't horrified that her son had had a manicure, she was delighted.

Nick nervously tucked his hand into the front pocket of his slacks.

When Kate looked around, it seemed like everyone had silenced and turned their attention to Nick. Half a dozen women, whose hats comprised a full rainbow of colors, instantly closed in on him.

"This is my son, Nicholas," Mrs. Atwood introduced him to the guests.

"It's Nick," he corrected her.

Kate felt his hand tighten around hers. Okay, so he was feeling a little stressed. He wasn't trying to hide behind her . . . yet.

"Mother." He pulled Kate forward by her hand and she wrapped his arm around her waist. "You remember Kate."

"Of course I do. We met last night," Mrs. Atwood said in a pleasant tone, loud enough for everyone to hear. "Your girlfriend."

The rainbow ladies in their organza, tulle, and chiffon-spun hats took a collective gasp and held their position. For the moment.

Nick had never been so angry with his mother. This was the third time she'd pulled him away from Kate. He liked it less and less each time it happened.

"I'd like to introduce you to Lydia Templeton. This is my son Nicholas." His mother beamed with more pride at every subsequent introduction.

"Call me Nick, please." He smiled at the woman and shook her hand.

"Lydia is a member of the Fine Arts League."

Fine arts? What did Nick know of fine arts? Symphony? Ballet? Opera? All subjects he had no interest in.

"I hear you live in the area?" Mrs. Templeton began.

Nick felt as if it were the first of many questions in her interrogation. He didn't know what she wanted him to tell her, but he could feel himself wanting to slip back into his shell.

"Yes, I do." Nick pinched his tie as if he were

straightening it. *SOS, Kate. SOS!* He glanced around, looking for her. He'd expected her to be nearby, listening in so she could help.

"Do you attend the opera, Nick?" Mrs. Templeton continued, sounding as if she were leading him somewhere.

"Not recently," was his polite answer. Then he spotted Kate standing way off to his side. There, she could see both him and the person he spoke to. To his surprise Kate wasn't staring at him but at Mrs. Templeton.

Kate touched her earlobe. *Talk to her.* What was he supposed to say?

"I just don't have . . . the time to attend as much as I'd like." Nick thought he'd talked himself out of a night at the opera pretty well.

Until Mrs. Templeton replied, "If you need an escort, I'm sure my daughter Antonia would be glad to accompany you."

Nick didn't mean he couldn't find anyone to go with, he meant he hadn't allocated time during his life to voluntarily attend.

"I can introduce you her to you, if you'd like."

Nick smiled and nodded, continuing to be polite as he'd been taught. Mrs. Templeton excused herself to find her daughter.

There was no one to blame but himself.

Not a minute went by before Nick's mother

brought another one of her friends for an introduction. Connie Kaminski.

Big surprise—she had a daughter who would be willing to accompany Nick to the museum's new art exhibit. If he just wanted to *see* her, it could be arranged.

Nick wanted to get away, but Kate signaled to him be polite and wait. He was very polite to Mrs. Kaminski, and when he saw the opportunity, he excused himself by saying, "I think I hear my mother calling."

With all things considered, Kate thought Nick was coping pretty well. She poured a cup of tea, helped herself to a biscuit, and sat on a wicker settee, keeping a watchful eye on Nick just in case he needed her again. Over at the next table she couldn't help but overhear the conversation.

"Shelby, who is that gorgeous man, over there in the gray pinstripe with his back to us?" All Kate saw of this woman was the back of her Apricot-colored, tulle-covered hat with silk bows.

"Can you believe that, Brit? You'd think Trish would recognize her own brother." Shelby muffled her giggle and exchanged coy glances with Brit from under the wide brim of her sky blue, flower-and-feather creation.

Trish? Brother? In less than a second, Kate had

puzzled out that Trish was short for Patricia, Nick's sister, who he called Patty.

"Nicholas? It can't be." Trish did a double-take and took two steps to the right, trying to get a better view. "Nicholas never attends Mother's—Oh, my goodness—it *is* him."

"Just introduce me as your best friend," Brit pleaded, adjusting her pastel yellow silk hat on her head. "It's the last thing I'll ever ask."

"Only after me," Shelby verbally elbowed in, knocking her hat askew.

"I'm not sure he's really available. He arrived with someone, you know," Brit interjected, throwing a wet towel on the subject of who-gets-Nick.

"As in a woman?" Trish looked as if she needed something stronger than tea to drink.

"Is she anyone?" Shelby intoned with her snobby nose held high. "No one *we* know."

Kate guessed because she wasn't a member of their *set*, she must have been one of the no-ones. This put Kate in a different position, and the spotlight was on her. In her case, wearing a hat would not have made the difference. Kate knew she did not fit in.

"Go ahead, with my blessings," Trish urged her two friends. Shelby and Brit secured their hats, left the table, and walked side by side toward Nick, not wanting one to step ahead of the other.

"They're in for a big surprise," Trish said. "Once a

geek, always a geek. I hope they're not too disappointed with him."

Apparently, Nick was right. His sister didn't think much of him. Kate was going to change that, right here in front of her eyes.

Nick couldn't help but smile when he saw Kate heading his way, an enchanting grin gracing her lips.

"Excuse me, ladies," she said, snaking her arm through his and pulling him away. "I hate to interrupt, but I need to steal Nickie for a moment."

"What is it?" Had he done something wrong? Had someone discovered he was faking? That he didn't belong here with the social climbers?

"I just wanted to make sure everyone believes you're as good as you seem." Kate's smile faded, softening her face, making her look vulnerable and sexy. "Touch my cheek."

"You want me to . . . okay." Nick stepped closer and cradled her jaw with his palm and brushed her cheek with his thumb.

He pulled his hand away and brushed his lips against her face with a gentle kiss. He didn't know why he did it, it just seemed like the thing to do. Nick wanted to do it. Her skin was soft and she had a fresh scent, blending into the garden flowers around them.

The rush of breath escaped her lips, much too

quiet to be heard by anyone but him. At that moment, he felt he was the center of her universe. Only the two of them stood there. He ran his hand up her spine, bringing her forward, leaning into him.

"Thank you," she whispered, running her hand along the lapel of his jacket. "You've just made me the envy of every woman here."

Kate stood alone again.

It wasn't like Nick was the only man there, because he wasn't. There were more than enough young men to attend to the young ladies. But somehow all the young ladies ended up congregating around her man.

The more mature crowd had been easy to cut through, but his groupies were changing, getting younger. The younger set had discarded their hats and were doing more hair-flipping and fluffing.

Kate's little tableau had made him the most desirable man there. The ladies fawned over him and must have had a silent pact to keep her from getting close and stealing him back.

Kate hoped he was doing all right. She couldn't get close to him except to see that he had shed his jacket and was down to his vest and shirtsleeves. But really, she shouldn't let those women corner him like that. Kate had to do her job and save him.

*   *   *

Nick heard his cell phone ring. "I'm sorry," he apologized while reaching in his pants pocket for his phone. "No one ever calls me." He pulled out his cell phone and motioned to the women to stay put as he moved away, mentally ticking off the number of people who had this number. "Hello?"

"Hello, Nick, it's Kate."

"Kate?" Nick glanced around, trying to catch sight of her. Wasn't she right here next to him? When had she left? "You're calling me on the phone? Where are you?"

"I'm in the house, looking at you from the kitchen window. Looks like you've got crowd control down pretty well."

Nick spied Kate through the garden window, standing at the sink. She waved.

"You've got quite a fan club there. Got them eating out of your hands, I see."

"I'm just putting what you taught me to work."

"I couldn't cut through your line of admirers. So I thought I'd try a subtle distraction."

Nick glanced back at the small gathering of women he'd just left. "Thanks."

"Do you need to be saved? Have you had enough?"

"Yes I have, and I'll meet you in the library. Just go through the door on the opposite side of the room and take the hallway to the end," Nick instructed her.

"I'll just make my apologies and tell them it's time for me to leave."

"And you thought that smooth line up all by yourself. It's amazing how well you're doing. You came up with that like a real pro. It looks like maybe you won't be needing me anymore."

Chapter Eight

Kate made it to the library first. Natural light poured in through the large wood-paneled windows, making this room as different as it could be from its dark-paneled nineteenth-century counterpart. The floor-to-ceiling book-lined shelves and welcoming, soft leather sofa and wing-backed chairs flanked a fireplace.

She strolled past the solid cherry desk and ran her hand over one of the chairs, the one near the far wall, facing away from the door. It wasn't hard to imagine a young, shy Nick curled up, immersed in a book, closing out the rest of the world that didn't understand him.

The sound of footsteps drew her attention to the

door. Nick stepped into the room and glanced over his shoulder as if checking to see if he'd been followed.

"Those ladies won't leave me alone," he said in a nervous rush.

"So I noticed." Kate didn't want to think of herself as the jealous type, especially not when it came to clients. But Nick was different from the others.

"I feel smothered. I think they wanted something from me, but I don't know what."

Kate knew exactly what they wanted. They wanted him. "They're all interested in you." Romantically. Like she was. Like she shouldn't have been.

"I want them to leave me alone."

Did he feel that about her too? Smothered?

"You aren't interested in any of them?" Many of the young ladies were very pretty.

"No, I—" He stopped and stared hard at her. "Aren't *we* supposed to be a couple?"

Explaining the complexity of couples was not only difficult, but Kate also found it awkward. "Yes, we arrived together, but they could think you're still up for grabs."

"I don't want to be *up for grabs*. I came here to practice interaction and conversation, not to find *another* girlfriend. Can we just tell them that?"

She could see he was feeling stressed by the way he raked his fingers though his hair. It was a new gesture; he probably hadn't done it while sporting a ponytail.

"I don't need the distraction. I have enough to deal with without them hovering around me. I can't concentrate on what I'm supposed to be doing." Nick ran his finger around his collar, adjusted his tie, and gulped.

"Keep thinking forward." Kate knew this was a struggle for him. He was taking three steps forward and two steps back.

"I just want to run away and hide." His voice sounded softer, weaker.

Unless Kate was very much mistaken, she thought she saw small beads of sweat on his forehead.

"I don't know if that's possible. I think they might follow you."

"I think you're right, and that scares me." He led her away from the window, closer to the chair near the bookshelves in what Kate thought of as "Young Nick's corner."

This time the corner seemed just the slightest bit dimmer than before and strangely comforting in the peaceful moment they stood quietly there.

"I spent a lot of time in here when I was young," Nick said in a soft voice. "I'd sit here and read while my father worked at his desk over there."

A spot in Kate's heart ached. How could she have

known? It was almost like she could feel echoes of his presence in the corner, in that chair.

"Even though it's been fifteen years since he's been gone, I still miss him."

"He was the only one who understood you?"

"He was the only one who ever sympathized with me. Life got more difficult after he died." Nick's melancholy moment dissolved, and Kate thought that somehow he was comforted by the chair. "Isn't there something you can do? To make things easier?"

"We have to show a united front." They could show blatant, explicit, outward affection for one another to chase the women away. But was it really necessary?

"A strong, united front. Good idea." He was totally buying into the idea. "How do we do that?"

"Make sure I'm with you, right next to you, at all times. Make sure you're holding my hand or have an arm around my waist, something that will demonstrate that we are together, a couple. That way—"

"A physical connection between us will tell the other women we're *committed* to each other." His eyes lit up. "They won't approach me while you're there. I see."

"Exactly." Kate had never heard it expressed that way before.

"What happens if—" Nick stopped and looked toward the door. "Someone's coming."

Kate didn't know how Nick knew, but by the look on his face she could tell he wasn't kidding.

"We'd better not be caught conspiring," she cautioned and wasn't sure where to go or what to do.

Nick pulled Kate against him, she slid her arms around his neck, and he kissed her—hard.

"There you are." Patty used that distinctive scolding tone of hers. "Mother and the guests were wondering where you were."

He pulled away from the kiss first, and if he had to guess, he'd say that he had surprised Kate but not in a bad way. There was a glow to her face, a softening of her eyes. The way she looked at him told him she enjoyed kissing him.

"Why don't you go back outside and I'll join you in a minute?" Nick whispered to Kate. He could tell by his sister's stance that there were more words to follow. Words he didn't want Kate to hear.

With Kate's cheery smile and the way her hand trailed the length of his arm and lingered just before she left, Nick had the feeling everything was going to be all right. He watched her walk away and knew things would be better than all right. Things couldn't be more perfect.

"I'm glad you managed to find someone to finally turn you around," Patty began in her approving tone, which wasn't much different than her disapproving one. "I hope you don't have any *serious* plans for her."

Nick pulled his attention from Kate and focused on Patty. "What do you mean?" He didn't like what she might be saying about Kate.

"I'm grateful to her that she, by some miracle, managed to make you presentable, but you can't think she could be anyone you'd ever think of marrying." Patty glanced down the hall, the way Kate had gone. "She isn't connected. There are better women out there who are dying to get acquainted with you. You shouldn't shut them out."

"I'm not interested in any of the *better* women," Nick replied, harsher than he had intended. Social standing wasn't everything. In Nick's book it meant nothing. There wasn't any *better* woman than Kate. Those women were just like his sister. All they thought about was social status, old money, and family connections.

"Having connections isn't everything." He started down the hall back to the party, then stopped and faced his sister. "Kate means more to me than you'll ever know. You don't know how lucky I am to have found her."

If looks could kill, Kate would have died the instant she stepped onto the back patio. The women had noticed she and Nick were both gone, all right. And she must have been radiating the sheer pleasure she felt welling inside her.

No one had ever kissed her the way Nick had. There was something about kissing him that made her insides melt. She grasped at the fleeting memory of his body against hers, firm and strong.

From the envious and determined expressions of the surrounding women, Kate sensed she had her work cut out for her; there was going to be a tug-of-war for Nick.

Only, she knew something they didn't. Nick was on her side. He wasn't the least bit interested in them, and the thought pleased Kate. His head wasn't turned by a bunch of women who were ultrathin with collagen-injected lips, silicon breast implants, and artificially-streaked hair.

And speak of the devil—Nick came strolling out of the house with his sister only minutes later. He walked right up to Kate and wrapped his arm around her waist, pulled her close, and nuzzled her neck in greeting just like he meant it.

It was a warm, comforting embrace. That was at first. Kate wasn't certain when it was that something changed in him, between them, but his whole demeanor shifted from mousy to magnetic.

Over the next hour, Kate saw him evolve into a well-spoken, articulate individual, discussing the details of the American Rainy Day Foundation.

Kate felt her willpower slipping as her admiration for him grew. As much as she tried to ignore her growing affection for him, there wasn't a thing she could do about it. She was slipping, falling, head over heels.

Nick had held onto Kate out of necessity but then, after the women had finally gotten the message and backed off, his touch had changed. His hands were firm but gentle, keeping hold of hers.

From desperate to dreamy.

He didn't have to keep her by his side anymore. Nick probably hadn't noticed the body language of the exasperated women when he foiled every attempt to separate them. He had held onto Kate like a lifeline, and Kate loved every minute of it.

It was almost as if he wanted her there, wanted to touch her. Leaning up against his side, Kate couldn't ignore the pleasure surging through her. She should have felt guilty about enjoying it but couldn't.

How attractive was a man who was blind to other women? A man who saw you and only you?

She leaned into him again and he gazed down at her, smiling. Hold on as she might, Kate felt the last of her willpower evaporate.

That was the moment when she fell in love with Nick.

He couldn't stop staring at Kate—looking at her, watching her, adoring her. He watched every glance, every smile, every move she made. Nick loved everything about her.

She checked her wristwatch. "We'd better leave if you want to meet Daniel on time."

"I don't want to leave." He didn't, and it all had to do with Kate. "I've had the best time this afternoon and I'm not ready for it to end."

"You were the one who didn't want to show up in the first place." She had every right to toss that at him. He had dragged his feet the entire way here, trying to talk her out of it all morning.

"I don't know how else to say this so I'll just say it." Could he look as confused as he felt? "I have to be honest with you." He stepped to one side and drew her close to him, whispered into her ear. "It's not my mother, the tea, or her guests. I don't want to go because . . . because I love being here with you."

He stared deep into her eyes and she stared back, unflinching, unblinking. They breathed as one, they were one in those few moments.

"Is it real? This . . . thing between us?" He paused, giving the low vibration of awareness time to pulse through her as it did him.

She felt it, didn't she? She had to.

"Is it real? I don't know if you ever could feel as I do. . . ." He stopped and wondered if he'd sounded like a complete idiot. "I have to know."

Could Kate lie to a man who was completely honest with her? He gazed at her, waiting for an answer. A truthful one.

The problem was, she could trust what he said because she knew he couldn't lie. Could she tell him how she really felt? What would happen to him if she told him? Nick was working so hard at changing, she didn't want do distract him with these new, unexpected feelings between them.

But could she lie to him?

"Yes, I feel it."

She'd never seen him smile as he did. His whole face lit up, glowed with excitement.

"Kate, that's wonderful!" He pulled her in close, right up to him. "What does this mean? What do we do about it?"

The questions came as a rush, and it didn't give Kate a chance to take in what was happening to them. How was she going to keep her mind focused and clear? And on track?

"Nothing," she finally said. "Look. You have to remember what you're doing, why you're here."

The expression on his face changed, not for the worse, just changed. Grew more serious.

"You have to remember that you have the fundraiser to think about."

She gave him a few seconds to let that sink in.

"I've got to admit that you've made astounding

progress in less than a week. You're the Miracle Man"—in more ways than one—"but you have another day and we're not letting up. You still have to work."

Nick nodded in agreement. It probably wasn't what he wanted to hear, and it wasn't what she wanted to say, but they couldn't stop and play kiss and tickle.

"We can't let the way we feel for one another get in the way. Not now. There's time after the fundraiser is finished."

Nick knew she was right. She wrapped her arms around his waist and looked up into his wonderful eyes. "I promise that three days from now we'll talk about this. All of this. About us."

Us. She liked the sound of that. And she couldn't help but smile. It felt good to be herself. Kate hadn't thought in terms of *us* for years, not since her deadbeat, good-for-nothing, lying, creepy, ex-boyfriends. She didn't want to ruin the mood or the way she felt by even thinking their names.

"It's just that right now isn't a good time. You understand, don't you?"

The range of emotions that flashed across his face went from confused to frustrated to knowing. As much as he wanted something to happen now, as much as they both wanted to explore this *thing* between them, it wasn't going to happen. Not just yet.

They had to wait.

"I agree. You're right, of course. But I can't help but feel—"

"I'm not asking you to forget your feelings. Just set them aside." Kate didn't want to wait either, but it was the smart thing to do.

"I can do that. It won't be easy, but I can do that." He moved away from her, putting some breathing room between them.

Kate wouldn't be taking this chance if it were anyone but Nick.

Honest, trustworthy Nick.

The man she could depend upon, the man she'd fought so hard not to love but fell in love with anyway.

And this time it was the real thing.

Chapter Nine

Kate knew that Nick had dropped her off at her office while he went to meet Daniel. However, she didn't remember leaving his mother's house or getting into his car or any details of the drive there. She was in a daze. A complete and total daze.

Things were happening so fast. She hardly knew him, but something deep inside told her he was the right one.

"Doctor O'Connor?" Raymond stood in her office doorway.

"Did you say something?" She blinked and made a real effort to pay attention to him.

"I asked if you needed anything before I left for the day."

"No, I'm fine, thank you." She hoped she looked

fine, too. All she needed was for detail-oriented Raymond to pick up that she was in love. It was personal. And Raymond didn't need to know anything about her personal life. "Nothing, thanks." Kate tried to steady her voice, sound as normal as she could. "I'm just here playing catch-up while I have some free time."

Raymond sauntered into her office and handed her several pink phone messages. "Nothing urgent."

"Good." She smiled up at him and got the distinct feeling he could read her mind.

He didn't know, did he? How could he? He didn't, Kate told herself. *There's nothing to worry about.*

Raymond held up a second stack in his other hand. "These are for Nick."

Kate felt her insides jolt at the mention of his name and hoped she hadn't shown any hint of reaction on the outside.

"I'll just hang on to them, then."

She chanced a look at him before he turned to leave and didn't see any hint of inquisitiveness on his part.

Kate relaxed in her chair in a state of euphoria. Everything concerning Nick had to stay professional and businesslike but just until the fund-raiser was over. After that she wouldn't have to pretend anymore.

Nick spotted Daniel at a table and took the seat next to him. "Caribbean Coolers, hey?"

"It's different." Daniel shrugged and pushed a large, tall cup toward him. "I was told to take you to different places, and this is my *different* choice of the day."

"I'm not complaining, just commenting." Nick tasted his smoothie. He felt great. Calm, unstressed, relaxed.

"Hey, there—it's *Nick* now, right?" Carl Kelly, the co-worker from the Gulf Coast who was living in Nick's house, held out his hand.

Nick pumped Carl's hand in greeting. "Yeah, that's right. Have a seat."

Carl pointed at Nick and eased into his chair. "What's with the suit? You're not interviewing, are you?"

Nick glanced down at his attire. He'd forgotten all about the suit he'd once griped about. "Oh, this. Went to my mother's this afternoon, met some of her friends."

"Your mother's?" Daniel's eyes widened. "She let you *talk* to her friends?"

"Surprising, isn't it?" Nick took a second sip of his smoothie. "I can't tell you how many things have changed in this last week."

"And what do you think *that* is?" Daniel spoke to Carl but discreetly pointed at Nick's face.

"It's a smile." Nick tried to behave as if nothing out of the ordinary were happening, but he wasn't sure he was pulling it off.

"No. I don't think so." Daniel overtly stared at him.

"I think—" Carl's eyes widened. "Wait a minute. I know what the look is. He's in love!"

Carl and Daniel laughed.

"So? What if I am?"

"I want to hear all about it." Daniel widened his eyes in interest.

"And I want to know who the lucky lady is." Carl shifted closer to hear the details.

"Her name is Kate." Nick had the feeling he might be acting silly, but there wasn't anything he could do about it. He couldn't help smiling.

"Kate who?" Carl shrugged. "Does she work with us?"

"You know Kate." Nick nudged Daniel. "Kate O'Connor. You're the one who introduced us."

"What?" Daniel choked on his drink. "Doctor O.? No way."

"I know, it's hard to believe but she lov—likes me. Me." It felt good to tell someone but after Nick let it out, he wondered if he should have. Then again, if he hadn't told someone, he was going to burst.

"But you two just met." By the look on Daniel's face it seemed that he was just as surprised as Nick had been.

"When did this happen? *How* did this happen?" Carl had been out of the loop. "Who's Doctor O.?"

"I'll tell you later," Daniel whispered to Carl.

"Last night, we bumped into my mother and she invited us to her tea party this afternoon. I think she did it because she thought Kate was my girlfriend."

"And what did Doctor O. think about that?"

"She thought it was a good idea to go . . . as sort of a dress rehearsal for tomorrow night. When I told her that my mother thought we were a couple she suggested we play along."

"She encouraged you?" Daniel sounded as if he didn't believe it.

"Insisted." Nick hadn't forced her.

"No kidding? And . . ."

"She wasn't my girlfriend. And at first I didn't like the idea of lying about it but then—" Nick paused and took a breath. "Something happened between her and me, and then it was real. We want to be together and I like it."

"You like it?" Daniel glanced at Carl. "What's there not to like?"

"Is she pretty?" Carl wanted to know.

"Beautiful, smart—Kate is such an amazing woman." Was it possible to list all her wonderful qualities? Nick didn't have time now but someday he would. He'd write them all down and use sheets and sheets of paper; the list would go on forever.

Daniel grabbed his cup, took a long drink, and looked away. "You and Doctor O. . . . who would have thought?"

"Nick and any woman," Carl added. "I needed to hear it to believe it."

"We've got to keep things quiet, just between us."

"Why the big secret? Things should be hot and heavy between you two right now." Carl chuckled. "You're in the discovery phase."

Nick took a deep drink and wished that things were hot and heavy between him and Kate. But they weren't, and waiting was for the best. He had to stay focused.

"We've shelved the whole thing until after the fund-raiser tomorrow night." Nick glanced at his watch. "As a matter of fact—"

"I thought we were supposed to work on polishing your social skills? Dealing with your comfort level, that sort of thing."

Nick looked from Daniel and Carl to the people milling about the store and didn't feel a twinge of anxiety. "My comfort level is fine. I have a feeling that from now on I won't have a problem interacting with anyone."

"Isn't it time to close up shop?" Nick was sort of surprised to see Raymond still at his desk when he arrived at The O'Connor Group office.

"Just cleaning up." Raymond tapped a stack of manila folders on his desk, straightening them. "These messages are for you."

Nick took the pink message slips from Raymond and glanced them over. "How did anyone know to reach me here?"

"Some people have their ways, you know." He tapped the side of his nose with his finger.

It seemed to Nick that Raymond was unusually quiet. Maybe he was waiting for Nick to say something. He had nothing to say, especially when it came to Kate. He'd probably said more than he should have to Carl and Daniel.

"Is there anyone you need to get back to right away?" Raymond stared pointedly at the messages in Nick's hand.

Nick glanced down at the messages and paged through them again. "I probably should."

"I hear you did well at the tea party." Raymond's voice was steady, calm, no indication of anything more than a causal conversation.

"Doctor O. was right. It was a good dress rehearsal."

"I can just see all the women lining up for you." Raymond stretched out his arm, staring past Nick, indicating the length of the line.

What was going on? Kate hadn't told Raymond, had she? About the women? About her? About them?

Nick didn't think so.

"I wouldn't say the women were lining up, but I spoke to a few. I found some of them difficult to deal with, but Kate took care of that."

"Difficult?" Raymond focused his full attention on Nick.

Nick glanced at Kate's office, making sure she wasn't within listening range. "Everyone there knew I brought Kate. But some of the ladies, my mother's friends, were working very hard to introduce me to their daughters. And there were my sister's friends who'd never paid any attention to me before but now insisted on speaking to me. It was different."

"You mean they were *hitting* on you?" Raymond rephrased more succulently.

"Yeah, hitting on me," Nick said confidently in Raymond's lingo. "As far as they knew, I was already taken." And that was the way Nick liked it.

"Well, that doesn't always matter with some women. Especially if you have what *you've* got."

"What have I got?" Nick glanced up at Raymond, confused.

Women had never shown any interest in Nick before. Had Raymond meant his Atwood family connections? His money? He personally didn't have much, and his future money was spoken for with the Rainy Day donation he'd made. Only him? That would really be a laugh.

"You've got a pretty wicked visual."

"A wicked what?" More new language that Nick didn't understand.

"Killer looks," Raymond rephrased for Nick's

benefit. "You're not too hard on the eyes. You're more than a good-looking guy, and by the sound of that line of women waiting for you, I'm not the only one who thinks that."

"I'm not concerned about my physical appearance."

"All women are."

"All women?"

"I'm sure Doctor O. is." Raymond said it like he knew it to be true.

"You think that Kate thinks I'm good-looking?" Nick didn't want Raymond to know that Kate was attracted to him. Did she consider him good-looking or handsome?

"She'd have to be blind not to think so. Why? You interested?"

"It's not my place to—" Nick had already told Daniel, and that was enough. Nick had to keep it to himself, keep his big mouth shut.

"Come on, you can tell me," Raymond urged, leaning forward, beckoning him near. "It'll be between just us men."

"I like her." Nick admitted. There was nothing wrong with telling the truth. However the *whole* truth was not going to come out.

"Like?" Raymond said distastefully. "I *like* her too, but I thought I sensed something more . . . a little *sizzle* between the two of you." He nodded. "There's definite chemistry there."

Was he trying to make something between them? Or was he trying to see if there already was something there?

"We work well together." Nick was not going to confirm any of Raymond's ideas.

"Work nothing. I'm talking about making some beautiful music, cooking big time, you know?"

"She is handy in the kitchen," Nick commented as nicely as he could about her kitchen talents. She, herself, admitted she didn't cook.

"Pah-leeze." Raymond laughed and rocked back in his chair. "Doctor O. in the kitchen? That's a good one."

Nick had the feeling there was more information coming out than he wanted. He needed to shut up and get out. He held up the messages, fumbled in his pocket for his cell phone, and backed away from Raymond's desk.

"I think I'm going to go call these people now."

Chapter Ten

Raymond buzzed Kate to tell her he was leaving and that Nick had arrived, waiting for her.

It was all she could do to remain calm. Just knowing Nick was here in the same office, on the other side of the wall, made her heart pound with anticipation and delight.

She had to keep her cool, keep reserved. It was for only one day.

One snail-crawling, second-by-second-dragging day.

Kate grabbed hold of the door knob and braced herself to see Nick. She would not bubble with excitement when she set eyes on him. She would only think about their working relationship and have Nick practice his social etiquette.

That's what tonight was for.

That's it. Only that.

Kate pulled open the door. Her breath caught when she saw him sitting in the waiting area.

Nick.

Still dressed in his suit. All gorgeous, handsome, and oozing maleness. His hair was just the slightest bit tussled. *Very sexy.* He had unbuttoned his collar and loosened his tie, giving him a corporate man's look: in control, in charge, and irresistible.

It was impossible for her heart to remain still, but she didn't have to let anyone know.

Kate put on her best cool, calm, and collected exterior and stood by the desk, waiting for him to get off the phone.

"Yes, that'll fit into my schedule. No, it's not a problem at all," Nick said into his cell phone. "Yes, I understand." He noted some information on a pad of paper. "That'll be fine. See you tomorrow."

He flipped the phone shut and set it on the desk.

"Hi," he said simply with a drop-a-girl-to-her-knees smile. It must have worked because Kate's legs felt wobbly.

"Who was that on the phone?" She leaned against the desk for support, hoping it would hold her up.

"That was the mayor's office." The way Nick looked at her was far from businesslike. "They're asking if I'll take some publicity photos at ten tomorrow morning." He pointed to one of the messages. "The Foundation wants me to attend a media pregala party at four to meet the director and the other board members beforehand." He pointed to another message. "I called this guy and left a message. I don't even know what he wants. And this one"—he pointed at a third message—"I can't call him back until eight tonight."

"Shall I cancel your gym workout tomorrow?" The mention of the gym brought a picture of Nick into Kate's mind that made her heart skip a beat. Why hadn't she kept her mouth shut?

"I'll see if I can reschedule. I find that working out relaxes me. It'll do me some good."

Another picture of Nick bulging and flexing . . . and smiling in a way she didn't want to think of.

"Raymond gave me this stack of messages. Why am I getting so many phone calls? And how did they get this number?"

Kate knew how the grapevine worked. His mother told a friend who told another friend and so on and so on. Some people knew other people who could find out things.

"Sounds like you're quite the hot property." Hot? Wrong word choice. She should really think about what she was going to say before she said it.

He gathered up his messages and slid them into his inside coat pocket along with his phone. "Everyone wants something from me."

Kate sighed. She wasn't any different. She did, too.

Nick had to get Kate some dinner quick. He noticed how she clutched onto the edge of Raymond's desk and figured it might be from hunger. He whisked her to a cozy diner called Boxcar.

"Are you sure this is where you want to eat?" If it were Nick's decision to make, he would have gone to a dimly-lit, semisecluded, romantic spot, just the two of them where he could be assured they'd not be disturbed.

"This is the perfect place. It has a friendly atmosphere and lots of people. It gives you another chance to learn to be comfortable around people."

The only person Nick wanted to be comfortable around was Kate.

Nick followed Kate and the hostess to their table. It wasn't too long ago that he was uncomfortable with the passing glances of the other people in the restaurant. It didn't matter, not anymore. The fleeting thought that it had once bothered him was almost laughable.

How much he had changed in such a short time. He went from unloved to loving Kate, and loving Kate made all the difference. What he really wanted to do was show up at her office with two dozen red roses and greet her with a kiss, a hug, and a smile—in that order.

Seeing Raymond at his desk when Nick stepped through the front door made him glad he hadn't done any of the things he had dreamed.

Kate was right. They needed to wait. Waiting until after the fund-raiser was finished would make life a whole lot simpler for both of them.

He couldn't help but want to lavish her, the woman he loved, with affection, attention, and flowers. But he had to wait. He would wait.

"See anything you like?" Kate asked, perusing the entrée selection.

"Definitely." But what Nick really wanted wasn't on the menu.

Being with her would have to be enough for the moment. For only a day more because that's all he—they—had to wait: one more day. But while he waited they could talk, laugh, and smile together. There was nothing stopping him from enjoying her company.

And there was nothing Nick liked better than being with Kate. If she wanted to sit in a family restaurant and have dinner, then Nick would gladly sit with her and enjoy every bite of the meal.

Was there anything he wouldn't do for her?

Nothing he could think of.

* * *

The Nick who sat across from Kate was not the same Nick who had strolled into her office nearly a week ago, nor was he the same Nick she'd gone to the tea party with that afternoon. This Nick was the more confident, assured of himself: a Nick that told her he loved her.

Even though they'd promised not to act on their feelings, Kate still felt strongly when she looked at him. Things had changed with him, things had changed with her, things had changed between them.

"I had a wonderful time today." Nick smiled adoringly, so she thought, at her. "I didn't think I would, but I did."

"You thought there was going to be a problem." The Nick of this morning might have thought so, but Kate didn't expect that this Nick would think the same.

"It's all because of you. My mother and her friends were all nice to me today. They all liked me, didn't they?"

"Yes, Nick. They did. Everyone liked you." She hoped it wasn't all going to his head. The attention and adoration of so many women might make a man think he's some kind of movie star. But not Nick.

Kate hoped not Nick.

"Everyone liked me, including you. Especially you." His smile was so sweet, it made Kate's heart ache. Of course he was right. She *especially* liked him, but that wasn't the point. "We weren't going to talk about this now, remember?"

"I remember." His fingertips brushed the back of her hand, sending waves of warmth up her arm.

"Are you ready to order?" a voice interrupted. Stephanie, the waitress, smiled and Kate could tell there was a bit of embarrassment when she asked, "Are you two newlyweds or something?"

Nick drove Kate home and walked her into the house.

"Newlyweds? She thought we were newlyweds." Nick still couldn't believe what their waitress had said.

"She wanted you to give her boyfriend lessons on being a boyfriend." Kate laughed and set her purse on her kitchen table.

"I don't have the experience for that yet, do I?" Nick leaned toward Kate. Close. "I know you're right about us not talking about . . . you know."

He stopped talking and she leaned toward him. There was a moment or two when he thought they might kiss. The way their breathing slowed, the way they looked at one another, staring deep into the other's eyes, the way they made the smallest move, closing the distance between them. . . .

Then Kate pulled back.

"Then let's not talk about *not* talking about it,

okay?" She took a deep breath and exhaled. "I never said I wasn't tempted by you. I just think we're better off concentrating on tomorrow night."

"You find me tempting?" No woman had ever said that about him before.

"Tomorrow night? Remember the Rainy Day fund-raiser? That's what all this is about." She gestured around her. "That's why you're here. That's why we're going through this." She softened her voice and glanced away from him. "That's why we're depriving ourselves."

"You feel as deprived as I do?" He wanted to know he wasn't the only one going through this torture.

"Maybe even more. Why do you think I didn't want to come home?" Kate reached to take Nick's hand. "Don't you think I know how difficult it'll be to say good-night? Without even a good-night kiss?"

Nick had never thought that far ahead. All he knew was that he didn't want to leave her.

"We both can be strong," she encouraged him. "It's only for one more day."

"I know you're right. I've been telling myself that you're right and you know what you're doing. But it's difficult."

She nodded. She understood.

"I want to kiss you and hold you so much. I want to—"

"I can't." Kate squeezed his hand, making him stop. "I'm suffering from a conflict of interest. You hired me, remember? I work for you. Acting any other way wouldn't be right."

"I understand."

"I have an obligation to you until tomorrow. After tomorrow, after the fund-raiser, we're regular people, and we can do what we want."

"Of course you're right. Completely. Will you come with me tomorrow, then?" He wanted her with him, next to him, near him. Nick would feel so much better knowing she were by his side.

"You go home and get a good night's sleep. You're going to need it for tomorrow." Kate straightened the ends of Nick's tie against his shirt. "Trust me, you can do this. The people there will love you just as they did today. You have nothing to worry about. I have complete trust in you."

"So . . . have you seen Nick at all today?" Raymond asked for the thousandth time the next afternoon when he strolled into her office for a batch of files. He was really getting on Kate's nerves.

"Still no, why do you ask?"

"It's just I'm not used to not hearing a peep from him. Don't you think it's a bit strange?"

"He's busy, Raymond. He's got a photo session, a luncheon, a press conference, several meetings, and a pre-party before the big party today. I think there's a chance we won't hear from him at all."

"Don't forget his workout with Ben," he added.

That refreshed the image of a hard-bodied, bulging, and flexing Nick in her mind. Kate didn't need that. She'd been dreaming of Nick all night and daydreaming about him all morning.

If Raymond knew what Nick was up to, then why did he have to ask her?

"I sort of miss him, don't you?" Raymond said in a cutesy voice.

"I hadn't even noticed." He was fishing for something but Kate wasn't going to bite. "Unlike you, I have work to do."

"I have work, too. I'm just saying that I've gotten used to having him around, that's all."

What did Kate have to say to keep him quiet? Would anything keep him quiet?

Kate closed the folder she was working on. "You know what? I think I'll just bring all this home and work on it there." If he wouldn't stop bugging her she could just put some distance between her and this busybody.

"You'll miss Nick if he comes in," Raymond crooned in a taunting tone.

"If he asks, you can let him know where I am, all right?" Kate said a little harshly. "As always, I'm available for emergencies."

"You got it."

Kate found herself packing up her briefcase in a matter of seconds. It didn't take long for her to realize that the reason she wanted to leave wasn't to get away from Raymond as much as she didn't want to miss seeing Nick.

She had been lonely for him. He had to go home to change before leaving. He might even be at Daniel's house this very moment, changing his clothes. Maybe even a shower.

Kate slammed her briefcase shut and hyperventilated.

Chapter Eleven

Kate didn't drive home; she drove to Daniel's house, hoping, praying, that Nick was still there.

"Nick! Nick? Are you here?" Kate rang the bell over and over in a panic.

He answered the door in his socks, a black bow tie slung around his neck and his shirttails flapping. "What is it? What's wrong?"

Kate stopped and stared. He wasn't sure what she was staring at exactly, but she was staring at him. She didn't look as if she'd been in a car accident, and the house wasn't on fire. Why did she sound so scared?

She swallowed hard and tried to catch her breath. "I wanted to see you before you left. I was afraid you'd gone."

"I'm glad you didn't." He let her in the house and pulled her into is arms for just a second before she stepped back.

"I'm sorry, I didn't mean to disturb you while you were dressing."

"That's all right. I can pick up where I left off." He finished buttoning his shirt. "The limo will be here in a half-hour. Let me get my shoes and jacket. I'll be right out, okay?"

Kate nodded.

A half-hour. That's all Kate had left with him.

"Are you sure you won't reconsider tonight?" He handed her his jacket while he sat to put on his shoes. "I really would like you to come with me."

"I can't. You know I can't. You have to do this. And I know you're going to make us both and your family proud."

Stepping in front of him, Kate detected a hint of spicy aftershave that he didn't normally wear, but in this attire and for this occasion it seemed appropriate.

Nick stepped back into the room fully dressed and completely stunning in his custom-tailored tux. He straightened his arms, adjusting the cufflinks.

"You're going to do great." She brushed at the non-existent lint on his lapels and straightened his bow tie. "I'll be waiting to hear all about your success."

"How about I take you out for breakfast and I can tell you then?"

"And you'll tell me everything?"

"Not one detail omitted. I promise."

"No oversleeping," Kate warned. "You've got yourself a breakfast date."

"This is it, then, isn't it?" His voice was tight. He was a little nervous, and he had reason to be. He was attending a big event. He had worked very hard to make a good impression.

"You're going to *wow* them," Kate smiled, hoping to give him a boost in confidence.

"You know what's really going to get me through tonight?" His eyes softened and he lost some of his nervousness. He touched her cheek and smiled. "Knowing that tomorrow is not just another day but *the* day."

The doorbell rang, several times. Someone pounded on the door.

"Kate! KATE!" More banging. "Kate!"

It had taken Kate forever to fall asleep. She woke fairly quickly. 3:27 AM.

"Kate!"

She knew it was Nick, but what he was doing here? Kate jumped out of bed and pulled on her robe. Nick practically fell in when she opened the door.

"You wait for me." He yelled out the door. "I'll be right back. You have to wait." Nick stepped into the house. "Oh, Kate. Kate!" He wrapped his arms around her and spun her around.

"Nick—Nick, put me down." Kate was afraid they'd both be taking a tumble. Instead, he ran wildly into the house before setting her back on her feet.

"Did I tell you? Did I?" He was more than just a little punchy. He was ecstatic, crazed.

"No, you didn't tell me anything."

"I was magnificent!" Nick started at her wide-eyed before jumping straight into the air. He told her about the people he met, how he shook their hands, posed for countless pictures, and made many quotable statements, all night long.

"Sounds like you were spectacular." Kate could not have been happier for him. "You see, you didn't need me there."

"I stood in front of those hundreds of people, and I knew what I was talking about." Nick roared with uninhibitcd laughter. "They thought so, anyway. I was good!"

"Are you drunk?" Kate blinked to clear her dry, sleepy eyes and looked at him a little closer.

"No, I can't drink. I've got to keep my head clear." Nick waved off any offers of alcohol he must have imagined from the invisible throng surrounding him.

"Nick? Are you okay?" Kate wrapped her arms

around him, trying to hold him steady. He was kind of wobbly on his feet.

"I'm good. Really. Good." He quieted, became calm and tucked his arm around her. Nick looked into her face and lowered his lips to her and kissed her.

Long, fulfilling, and completely satisfying. Kate leaned into him and let loose every inhibition. When they ended their kiss she'd expected him to say something warm, wonderful. She didn't know, something unexpected, something that would surprise her.

"Maybe this wasn't a good idea that I come here." Talk about backpedaling, Nick was actually walking backward away from her.

That wasn't it.

Then he stopped. "Kate," he said. "Kate."

She stared at him and waited.

"I think I'm a little tired."

"I think you might be exhausted." It was difficult to see him clearly in this light, but he was beginning to look—

"Yeah." His eyes rolled back and he collapsed onto the sofa.

Kate rushed to his side and checked that he was still breathing. She didn't have to get very close. His snoring told her that he had fallen asleep.

A car door closed, and Kate remembered the limo and its driver. She ran to the door and called him in to help.

"Nick? Wake up."

"Sir?" the driver helped Nick sit. "Mr. Atwood? Let's take you home, sir."

"Home." Nick yawned. He was as cooperative as one could expect with a shovelful of Mr. Sandman's dust in each eye. Once he was in the limo, Kate kissed Nick's cheek and closed the door.

Inside her house, Kate threw the deadbolt on the front door before heading to the phone to call Daniel.

"Sorry it's so late—early—but Nick's in a limo on his way home. Could you make sure he gets safely to bed? And tuck him in for me, will you?"

The next morning, Nick took Kate to a small diner where the food was good and the waitress just seemed to know when you wanted something. It wasn't nearly as romantic as the candlelit dinner he had envisioned the night before, but it didn't really matter as long as he was with Kate.

"You were exhausted when you came by last night. You should have canceled breakfast and slept in." Kate glanced over the breakfast menu.

"Hmm. I'm glad to know that I looked as bad as I feel." Sleeping in would be what Nick needed to feel one hundred percent, but he wasn't willing to give up a chance to see Kate. "I would never miss seeing you if I could help it. Thank you for not leaving me in the driveway."

"I certainly couldn't leave you outside in the snow in the middle of the night." Kate set her menu to one side and turned her coffee cup right side up.

"It was the middle of the night, but it wasn't snowing. It was a balmy seventy degrees." Nick placed his menu on Kate's.

"You know what I mean." She shrugged and they smiled at one another.

Kate ordered English muffins and coffee while Nick decided on a cheese omelet. So much for a romantic breakfast.

"Other than being universally loved and an overwhelming success, do you remember anything else about last night?"

"Ah . . . I believe I agreed to become the spokesman for the Foundation. They've assigned one of their publicists to me to help with the media offers."

"How many offers?" Kate didn't sound as if she liked his big idea.

"Several." Nick tried to remember the ones he could. "Local papers want to do follow up, and some local television stations were interested. I'm supposed to be a guest on one of the radio talk shows in L.A. next week."

"What about us?" Kate's smile had faded altogether. "It sounds like you're going to be gone a lot."

"Just for a while, but nothing is going to change between us. I promise." And nothing would change for him; his feelings would not change. Nick smiled at her, hoping to give her some of the confidence he felt.

Their breakfast arrived, distracting them momentarily.

"Are you moving back to your mother's?" Kate asked.

Nick glanced up at her. His appetite seemed to be waning, and he alternated pushing his hash browns away from one side of his plate to the other.

"I can't just move in with you. We really don't know one another that well." Their first day together wasn't turning out as joyful as he had expected.

"I know." Of course she knew. "We need time."

"It's just that . . ." He touched her arm so she'd look at him. Her eyes were moist, close to tears. "When it comes time to live under the same roof together, I want to do it right. I want us to be married."

Nick wanted to marry her?

That came as sort of a shock. Kate hadn't thought that far ahead. And it was hard to believe that Nick had even considered it. Neither one of her ex-boyfriends had, even after two or three years of dating.

"We haven't really begun," Nick continued. "We're just starting our life together. It might be bumpy for a while, but we've got to hang in there."

The tables had definitely turned—look at who was giving the pep talks now.

"We both have things to do today. I'll meet you tonight for dinner, all right?" There was no hesitation in his voice, he wasn't trying to pacify her. "No family style, crowds, or friendly atmosphere tonight. It's going to be you and me and one little candle, just bright enough so I can see your beautiful, smiling face."

How could she refuse? How could Kate ever think that things were over between them? Maybe there was some bumps in the road as they started out, but who cared?

As long as they were together.

After breakfast, Kate went straight to her office. Raymond had handed her a stack of messages before she even had a chance to sit at her desk. Her regular clients were lining up, begging to see her.

Nick was right. She was busy, and she had to get back on track and see to business.

The morning hours blended into the afternoon, and it wasn't until two that Raymond had pointed out she hadn't had lunch.

"Let me run out and get you something," he offered.

Eat now and ruin her appetite for dinner? It didn't matter; dinner was to be with Nick. It wasn't like they were going to dig into roast beef and baked potatoes.

"Just a nonfat latte and a lowfat scone." Kate gave in. That wouldn't ruin her appetite.

The phone rang the second after Raymond left,

and Kate couldn't have been happier to hear Nick's voice on the other end. With Raymond gone, she could speak freely. A little cutesy talk over the phone would be embarrassing if overheard.

"I'm really sorry, Kate," Nick repeated a number of times. "The reservations are already made. I was really looking forward to this evening, spending time with you. But I have to fly out tonight. I would have never agreed to any interviews for—"

"It's all right. You have to go. There's nothing you can do about it, is there?" Kate couldn't help but feel disappointed. She'd been looking forward to seeing him.

"I just want you to remember that nothing has changed," were his last words.

Yes, nothing had changed.

Nick was gone, and Kate was still alone.

Chapter Twelve

It was Saturday, 7:20 PM.

Kate stepped inside the front door of her house. It felt as empty as she felt inside.

Nick was really gone.

She was beginning to wonder if she'd ever see him again.

What was it about Nick anyway? How could he have gotten to her like that? What was it about him that seeped under her skin and wound around her heart and made her feel incomplete with his absence?

Kate had the worst feeling. Things weren't going to get better, she just knew it. She dashed away the tears that had dared to roll down her cheeks.

It was over between them even before they'd started. They had said their good-byes that morning at breakfast, but Kate couldn't get over the feeling that it really was good-bye forever.

It was Sunday, 7:19 AM.

Kate answered her home phone.

"Hello? Kate?" Nick sounded stressed and out of breath.

"Nick, how are you?"

"Rushed. I'm running through the Denver airport. We're headed to the other side of the terminal"—he paused and Kate heard the shuffle of footsteps—"for the connecting flight to O'Hare."

"Chicago?" He was physically moving farther away.

"Come on! Come on!" A man shouted. "They're holding the plane for you."

"I've got to go, love you." Click.

Kate pulled the phone away from her ear. At least he still loved her.

Kate powered on her cell phone on her way out the front door Monday morning. It beeped, saying it had a voicemail waiting.

"Sunday, ten fifty-eight PM," the voicemail lady announced.

"Hi, Kate. It's nearly one in the morning, and I wanted to call but didn't want to wake you. I'm hoping that this craziness ends soon, and I can come home. I'll call you again when I can." There was a longish pause. "I just wanted you to know how much I missed you. 'Bye."

Kate hung up.

At least he missed her.

How could Nick not find the time just to call at a decent hour?

It was Tuesday, and Kate found it hard to concentrate on what she should be doing. She kept replaying the week she'd spent with Nick in her head. Was any of it real? Had there ever been any attraction between them?

It was difficult to say, now that he was gone.

She seemed to remember . . . yes, there was. Thinking back on it now, it felt like it was all a dream.

"I wonder what Nick is doing right now?" Raymond queried with a sigh.

"I really haven't thought much about it." Kate took the folders she'd asked for and handed him another folder to file.

"Don't you even try to deny that you don't think he's someone special."

"Special?" Where had Raymond picked that up? She'd never give any indication that Nick was anyone other than a regular client.

"Well, I've never heard of you cooking dinner for anyone before." The comment sounded more like a rhetorical question. "I was under the impression that you couldn't even cook."

"I wasn't cooking."

"You were helping."

"I . . ." Why did she even bother defending herself? "How do you know?"

"Nick told me," Raymond let the confession slip like it was some grand secret.

Exactly how close were Nick and Raymond?

More important, what did Raymond know about Nick that Kate didn't?

It was Tuesday, 9:38 AM.

"Doctor O., Nick's on line two," Raymond announced on the intercom.

Kate punched the button and pressed the phone to her ear. "Nick?"

"I'm so glad I got a hold of you. The Foundation has me running a maze. It's all I can do to get a few hours of sleep."

"You know how dangerous that can be. Who knows whose driveway you'll end up on." They shared a genuine but awkward laugh. "Where are you now?"

In the fifteen seconds of silence Kate could hear the rumble of road noise.

"Manhattan."

"New York?"

"I'm sorry. I've got to go." Nick sounded sad. "I

want you to know that I think about you all the time." Click.

Well, at least he thought about her.

It was Wednesday, 9:56 AM.

"Nick is going to be on *Brandish and Blair TO-DAY*!" Raymond announced, bursting through the door an hour later. "We can watch it here." He opened the cabinet door that hid the television in her office and promptly made himself comfortable on the sofa.

"Come on, Doctor O. Sit by me." Raymond patted the spot next to him.

With mixed emotions, Kate made her way from behind her desk to the sofa.

"Hurry, you don't want to miss him."

Miss him?

Kate sighed. It was way too late for that.

"Raymond—"

He shushed her. "They're talking about him—listen."

Raymond used the remote to turn up the volume and stared wide-eyed at the television screen.

"Did you see this?" Will Brandish picked up a magazine off the table. "Nick Atwood, who's here today, on the cover of *NewsMakers Weekly*." Brandish held it up, but the camera couldn't get a good shot of the cover.

Nick was on the cover of *NewsMakers*? Kate had

no idea. The urge to run out and buy every copy she could find was overwhelming, but she'd never ask Raymond to do it.

"Let me see." Blair took the magazine from Brandish to take a look. "Great cover."

"Do you think he always has that rainbow aura over his head? Look—look at him." Brandish pointed at the cover.

"I don't know." Blair finally held up the magazine for the camera.

"Oh, my gosh! It's really Nick on the cover of *NewsMakers*," Raymond gushed. "I'm going out to get one during my lunch break."

On the cover, Nick held an umbrella to protect him from the rain and gazed in the distance at the emerging rainbow with its legendary pot of gold.

"Did you see him backstage before the show?" Blair pushed the magazine aside.

"You know I go straight from my dressing room to this chair. Car—dressing room—chair. That's it." Brandish punctuated every word in an exaggerated, overly-dramatic style, and the audience laughed. "I meet the guests when they come out here. That's the whole purpose of the show, isn't it?" He shrugged then looked off camera. "Am I right?"

The audience laughed again.

"Let me tell you, Brand." Blair stayed her cohost's outburst by laying a hand on his arm. "I'm a married woman, happily married woman, but that guy, Nick . . . well, let's just say that he *is* a hottie."

"Hottie?"

"Oh, yeah. Big time." Blair fanned herself with her notes. "He's got that smart, good-looking, charm thing working for him. You know what he does, don't you?"

"Who cares what he does if he's a hottie." Brandish shrugged, making fun of Blair, and the audience laughed.

"He makes my toes curl," Blair added, rolling her eyes. She licked her lips with an exaggerated slurp. "Yummy. I hope my husband isn't watching this."

"Let me get this straight, Nick Atwood's a *yummy hottie* and I'd better concentrate on keeping my toes straight."

"He might not affect you that way, Brand, but I'm telling you, you'd better watch out."

Brandish laughed and pointed to the camera. "And we'll meet this Nick Atwood when we come back."

The show's music played for a few seconds, and Raymond muted the TV while the first commercial aired.

"He'll know to dress up, won't he? A jacket? Or is he planning on wearing a suit?" Raymond rambled through his questions without giving Kate a chance to answer. "He didn't call me. Did he call you?"

No, he hadn't.

"Will you just calm down, Raymond?" Kate needed to take her own advice. With each passing minute her stomach turned cartwheels, and they soon turned into handsprings, and the anticipation of seeing Nick was building to an uncomfortable, intolerable level.

Watching him on TV was far from seeing him in the flesh, but at the moment she was feeling a bit desperate. *Abandoned* was a better description.

Cut off from him . . . Kate had been Nick-less for days.

"You might be surprised that we're having this young man out first. He isn't a big movie star, and he isn't even really famous," said Brandish.

"Not yet!" Blair interrupted, overenthusiastic.

"But Blair likes him, and from what I hear this personable young man is here to talk to us about an important cause. Here he is, Nick Atwood." Brandish gestured to his right and the camera followed.

Nick stepped out, smiled, and waved to the audience. He shook Brandish's hand, then Blair's, and sat in one of the tall, swivel chairs next to them.

"Hi there, Nick, how are you doing?" Brandish asked.

"Fine."

"You're from California, right? Is this your first trip to New York City?"

"Yes, it is. This is very different from where I'm

from." Nick flashed a smile, and Kate could swear she heard some of the audience members swoon. "I like it."

"Oh, my gosh. Doesn't he come across as a total hunk?" Raymond whispered.

"He looks great," Kate commented coolly, and Raymond shushed her again. She'd never let on how wonderful he looked to her.

Kate knew how being the center of attention made him nervous. Nick looked calm, totally unfazed by the camera and audience.

"So tell us what you're here to talk about," Brandish began. "And what did you choose to do about it? Because you did make a very conscious, deliberate choice."

"All I did was make a donation to the American Rainy Day Fund."

Blair elbowed her cohost. "But it wasn't just any donation, Brand. He donated his salary for what—a year, two? I heard that totals up to nearly half a million dollars."

"I tried to keep my contribution anonymous." There was a flash of the old, adorable, self-conscious Nick who Kate had known so well.

"Why would you want to do that?" Blair shrugged like the whole concept was the dumbest idea in the world.

Nick told the rest of the story, about working with

his team before the flood, the effects of the flood, and what he did, as only one person, to help. He made a donation to the Foundation, brought a family from that area, and provided a home.

Then he spoke about his employer encouraging employees to make donations and then matching the company-wide contributions, an idea that caught on with other Silicon Valley companies. Finally, he told them about the mayor of San Francisco getting involved for the fund-raiser, which turned out to be a major West Coast event.

"That's wonderful. We'd all want to be involved with something that would make a difference." Brandish nodded, agreeing with Nick. "You've been on Chloe's show, is that right?"

"We taped the show a few days ago. They said it was going to air next week."

"The whole reason for your appearance here and on Chloe is because you want to bring this cause and the Rainy Day Fund to public attention."

"There are people who, every year, lose their lives, family members, homes to natural disasters. Earthquakes, floods, mudslides, tornados, hurricanes, drought, ice storms—we're at the mercy of Mother Nature, and we have to be prepared for the ride. The Rainy Day Fund helps those affected pick up the pieces after something like this."

Blair wiped at the corner of her eye. "It's a great

cause, and all of us should congratulate you for showing such dedication and support."

"Glad to meet you, Nick." The camera came in close on Brandish, and he slipped out of his chair to shake Nick's hand before he left. "Next up," he said to the camera. "She's got a new movie out and she's breaking hearts—the very lovely, the very talented, Judith Lonsdale."

After the Brandish and Blair show, Nick hardly had time to breathe. He was rushed from one place to another, had to meet with this important person, then that one.

Everyone he met during this media tour took an instant liking to him, something that never used to happen as his old self. He was wary of people who cozied up to him. Newfound friends and women hitting on him were common occurrences.

The longer he'd been away from Kate, the more he began to wonder if she was like the other women, preferring the new Nick to the old Nick.

Maybe what he thought had happened between them never happened at all. Maybe she didn't love him, the real him. Maybe Kate was in love with the Nick of her creation.

Maybe he was making it all up in his head.

They'd handed him a wrapped burger and a soft drink and shoved him in the back of a limo. Nick figured this meant he was going to be in there a long time. Chris, his publicist, talked one hundred miles a minute, much faster than Nick could listen, about updates on where he was going, who he'd meet next, and then what new TV show, magazine interview, or other promotional dance he'd be doing.

Nick was tired. All he wanted to do was hear Kate's voice. On second thought, if she'd been here in the back of this limo instead of Chris, he'd be very happy indeed.

Chris had finally stopped talking to Nick and was now busy talking on the phone. Nick had no idea how long he had, but he knew he had a few minutes to himself. He pulled out his phone and flipped it open.

The buttons were blurry, and he blinked to clear his vision before punching Kate's number. He pressed the phone to his ear and closed his eyes. He drifted into thought of the soft, warm scent of her hair and the ethereal feeling of gazing into her eyes. So nice . . . so nice. . . .

"Hello?" Kate said. "Hello?"

Chapter Thirteen

It was Thursday, 1:47 AM.

Kate replaced the phone receiver. She decided against leaving him a message and lay back onto her bed. No, she shouldn't call him. It was late, and there was no telling where he was at this time. What she was really afraid of was finding out which woman he was with.

He had a new life to go along with his new fame. In a few weeks' time she wouldn't be surprised if he had forgotten all about her. About what they had, or what she thought they had. Clearly it was only her imagination.

Maybe she'd made the mistake in thinking he never looked at other women, that she was or would be the only woman in his life.

Inside, in her heart, she held on to the notion that Nick was different than anyone she'd ever met. But holding on to that thought was tearing her apart.

Was she willing to wait? And for how long?

Friday, 8:18 AM, Kate rolled over in bed and looked at the clock. She'd overslept. The extra hours didn't make her feel any more rested. She'd spent the night tossing and turning, unable to sleep, unable to think of anything, anyone, but Nick.

She had her work, her clients. Her whole schedule was put on hold because of him, and she needed to get her company rolling again.

After stepping out of the shower, Kate turned on the TV to find, instead of the morning news' status on the commute, Beth Jenkins was introducing Nick on *Sunrise in America*.

Nick had rushed from the airport to The O'Connor Group office only to have Raymond hold up his hand for Nick to wait and remain quiet while he spoke into the telephone headset.

It was all Nick could do to stand still in front of Raymond's desk. He didn't want to wait. He wanted to see Kate now.

Sooner than now.

Nick kept glancing at the office door, waiting, hoping for Kate to poke her head out to see who was here. He knew she was inside, she was always in before eight in the morning.

"All right," Raymond said with certainty, jotting notes on a message pad. "Okay. Yes, I understand."

"I was hoping to catch Kate. I know she usually comes in by eight."

"Not today, she hasn't come in yet this morning," Raymond said in his precise enunciation.

Nick hadn't had a chance to see or speak to Kate since he'd left. He'd missed her so much, and he wondered if she had missed him at all. He'd called her every chance he'd had. He hadn't heard from her. He figured that seeing him in person was far better than calling her on the phone.

Meeting her face to face, he'd find out what was going on and how they really felt about one another.

"I'm sorry I missed her." What was he going to do? He couldn't stay.

"Would you like to wait?" Raymond motioned to the seats in the waiting area.

Nick glanced at his watch. It was getting late. "I can't. I have a flight." Nick glanced at the front door, hoping she'd come bursting in. "Will you tell her I stopped by?"

"Sure. I'll let her know. When will you be back?"

"I'll be on the East Coast until the middle of the week." He tried to recall what exactly was going on, but in his rush nothing was coming to mind. The publicist took care of all scheduling and only told Nick what he needed to know for the next couple of days.

"More TV appearances? I've tried not to miss any. I don't think I have, not a single one." Raymond sounded more like a boy band groupie than an administrative assistant.

"I figure it's more publicity for the Rainy Day Fund."

"You'll let me know when to tune in, won't you?" Raymond shook his head. "Forget it, I'll call your publicist, Chris."

"You know Chris?" Nick didn't have time to try and figure that out. "What I really came by to do was drop off the cell phone you loaned me." Nick pulled his cell phone out of his pocket and held it out to Raymond. "Got my own." He patted the breast pocket of his jacket. "Let me give you the number just in case you or anyone might need to get in touch with me." He handed Raymond his business card with his new cell phone number.

"I'm sure *anyone*"—Raymond waggled his eyebrows—"will be interested in having it."

Kate walked into her office at 10:30, and she was in a bad mood. She got a late start, which made her late to the office. To top if off, Raymond wasn't at his desk when she arrived. But those weren't the real reasons why she felt like chewing a box of nails. She'd been in a constant bad mood since Nick had left.

Kate was angry that he hadn't called. She was angry that it made her angry, and she was especially angry at herself for not being able to get over it.

He was gone. And that was that.

Raymond stepped into her office and announced, "Nick was just here. About five minutes ago."

"Nick was here?" The one day Kate was late to work.

"I figured you'd need these because you'd be starting the day off badly." Raymond held up the tall, nonfat, double decaf, 180 latte in one hand and a Snickerdoodle in the other. He was wearing the most disgusting, cheery smile she'd ever seen. "Because you missed him."

Excited that Nick had stopped by and cursing her luck that she had missed him, Kate kept her composure. "I could care less." She didn't want Raymond to know how hurt she felt. Heck, she could barely admit it to herself, and only in the dark with the door closed.

"Really?" He set the morning nosh on her desk and headed back for the door. "Have it your way."

"What did he want?" she did her best at keeping her voice even.

"He just dropped off his loaner phone." Raymond

pulled the familiar-looking ultrathin cell phone from his pocket.

Without a word, Kate snatched it from him.

"Would you like—"

"No—I don't want to be disturbed." And she slammed the door behind her just as the tears began. Big, fat wet tears ran down her face.

He'd gone, and he couldn't care less about seeing her. He'd stopped by to drop off his phone and that was it. He didn't care about her at all. Maybe that was pessimistic thinking, but that's the way Kate felt. She'd never felt worse in her life.

Nick's cell phone rang. Kate flipped it open.

"Hello," Kate answered the phone tentatively. Again, anxiety coiled in her stomach, hoping it was Nick.

"Is Nick there?" a woman's voice, sounding vaguely familiar, said.

"No, he isn't."

"Oh, well." A pause. "Can you tell him to call Judy—Judith when he has a chance? He has the number."

Kate wasn't sure he even knew a Judy or a Judith. "Judy who?" Kate wondered with an aura of jealousy that began to strengthen.

"Lonsdale."

Judith Lonsdale the actress? "Sure." Kate's voice

grew hard and cold with jealousy. "I'll tell him when I see him."

"It took forever to get his number. Thanks so much." Kate flipped the phone closed. If Kate thought she felt bad when she came in, now she was scraping the bottom of the emotional barrel.

Kate paused at Raymond's desk when his phone rang later that afternoon. Not that she was waiting for Nick to call—she was certain that would never happen. She was curious to see which other celebrities were interested in Nick.

Raymond picked up the phone receiver: "The O'Connor Group." He sat quiet for a moment, listening to the other end of the line.

"No, I am not one of Nick's *people*, but if you leave a message I'll make sure he gets it." Raymond jotted the name and phone number on a pink message pad.

"Was it Judith again?" Kate rolled her eyes, trying to keep her green-eyed monster at bay.

"No, Guinevere Baker," Raymond said matter-of-factly, filling out the date and time on the pink note slip.

"I'm surprised Holly Russell hasn't called yet."

"She called just before you got here." Raymond glanced at his watch. "Look at the time! We'd better flip *Chloe* on or we'll miss him."

Raymond pushed away from his desk, shot out of his chair and dashed toward Kate's office.

"Don't tell me—" Kate could scarcely believe it could be true. No wonder he'd forgotten all about her. He was busy with the beautiful starlets in his new circle of friends, his Hollywood circle.

"Quick, let's turn on the TV in your office, Nick's on the Chloe Sanders show today!"

The introduction music to *Chloe* played just as Kate sat next to Raymond on the sofa. Raymond had efficiently turned on the TV and tuned into the right station before she had the chance to get comfortable.

Right after the first commercial, Chloe introduced Nick. He looked as natural as he could, sitting next to her: poised, confident, sexy.

Chloe swiped at her chin. Was she drooling? It was bad enough how Blair Calloway went on about Nick, but Chloe? Kate thought she had more class than that.

Inside, Kate still felt that sense of pride. She was glad they loved him. Everyone loved the outgoing, charming, charismatic Nick. But she knew that no one loved Nick the way she had. Nor did anyone love the same Nick that she did.

"Well, that's it for today." Raymond clicked the TV off. "I think we've had our daily Nick fix."

She had to bite her tongue to prevent herself from

telling Raymond that he had to speak for himself because Kate hadn't had enough of Nick. Not by a long shot.

"And just think you missed getting his autograph this morning. But don't worry." He patted her on the shoulder. "I have a feeling he'll be in touch again."

But Kate wouldn't let herself care. She was numb from the ache, and she didn't want to feel this way anymore.

And she wouldn't. She couldn't. She had to do something to make the hurt stop.

Kate was jealous. Plain and simple. Not of what he had or who he was, but where he was and who he was with. The local socialites who pursued him at his mother's tea party would be nothing compared to the national exposure. There was no telling to which woman he would appeal next.

Kate found the videotape he'd made nearly three weeks ago. She slid it into her machine and hit play. With the tape she found his old clothes. She pulled out the T-shirt, the tired old jeans, and the stupid sandals.

"We'll start with your name," she heard her voice from off camera.

The nerdy Nick glanced around, and she could sense how uncomfortable and self-conscious he felt. Her heart ached when she caught sight of the occasional familiar expression, gesture, or the tilt of his head.

It was still him. Even back then.

Kate held the shirt to her face and inhaled. His scent, still the same. She couldn't help but smile when she saw the raw beginnings of who he was today. Yes, he was the same, just more refined. He had found his true self—his inner man. She may have helped, but he'd done the work. No one could change unless they wanted to.

Looking at the videotape, she could still see the Nick she had fallen in love with. He was just hidden under his shield of shyness, unwilling to show the world who he was. Or afraid to because they wouldn't like what they saw.

At that time she hadn't recognized his tenderness and charm. Now, Kate couldn't see anything else.

Watching the nerdy Nick on the tape made Kate miss him all the more; she wanted to have him there, not just an image, but the real flesh-and-blood man.

She could understand he had more important things to do. He had gone places, moved beyond her. And she wondered if he thought about her at all. After all, she had gotten him started on this path.

And he'd probably been too busy to say thank-you. She even wondered if he remembered the spark between them.

There had been one, once.

Chapter Fourteen

Over that weekend there were nine mystery calls. Sometimes there was just no one on the other end of the line. Sometimes there was a kind of cryptic, ghostly voice mumbling in the background or the shrieking of women's laughter. One time there was just loud snoring.

Not that Kate kept count, but there were five on Saturday and four on Sunday.

There was no way Kate could compete with any of the women interested in him now. And if that's the kind of woman he wanted, fine.

Kate's depression was turning into anger. Maybe he was off with Judith or Holly or maybe Guinevere. Who cared?

Nick didn't owe Kate anything. And she'd be

happy to forget all about him. But the problem was, everywhere she looked, all she saw was Nick. Nick in the newspapers, Nick on the radio, Nick in magazines, Nick on the TV.

Nick. Nick. Nick.

Wasn't there any other news besides Nick Atwood? Something in the world more newsworthy must have happened, something other than Nick-related.

Friday night, he was on some late-night talk show, and he had a political roundtable discussion Saturday morning. By Sunday, Kate was completely sick and tired of him. Hadn't he heard of overexposure?

If Nick wanted to be a bicoastal publicity monger, he could go ahead and hobnob with the movers and shakers, rub shoulders with the rich and famous. Kate didn't care.

She was tired of hearing about Nick second- or third-hand, of seeing him somewhere else other than here with her. She turned off the television and decided if he was really out of her life she had to make the effort to keep him out.

Completely. No more Nick.

Monday, 7:58 AM: Kate marched into her office and stopped in front of Raymond's desk.

"See all these messages for Nick." Raymond laid his hand on a pile of pink papers.

"Nick who?" Kate widened her eyes, acting as if she hadn't a clue who Raymond was talking about.

"Nick—you know." Raymond paused, clearly confused by her reaction, then laughed like she was being silly.

"This office is not the headquarters of the Nick Atwood fan club." Kate scooped up the pile and dropped them in the trash. "We have a business to run here, and if it weren't for Mr. Atwood in the first place we wouldn't be scrambling around, playing catch-up."

"But won't Nick—"

Kate held up her hand, stopping Raymond from any more hero-worship praises. "I don't want to hear another word about him—unless it has to do directly with this office or this business specifically. Is that clear?"

"Crystal, Doctor O'Connor." Raymond dropped any frivolity in his voice and snapped back into his normal all-business demeanor.

"I'll be in my office waiting for my next appointment." The real reason she went to her office, and closed and locked the door behind her was to channel-surf. She wanted to find which show Nick was on this morning so she could have the satisfaction of turning it off.

* * *

Monday, 8:48 PM: What was the use of going home? She couldn't hide from him there, either. Preventing any and all kinds of information about Nick was harder than Kate thought. She'd done it, but it wasn't easy.

Kate changed out of her work clothes and pulled on her blue robe. Wrapping it around her and tying it closed with the belt was a far cry from Nick's loving arms. She wanted warmth and comfort, but this was the best she had.

She turned on the kitchen TV and flipped to a cable news station to get the "top 10 new stories in 20 minutes" and opened the refrigerator for something to eat.

Kate fought the thoughts of Nick trying to work their way into her consciousness. If she had to rate how she had done, she would have claimed victory.

That was until she opened the freezer door.

Kate pulled out an aluminum foil block sealed in a plastic freezer bag. She didn't have to have X-ray vision to know what it was.

It was lasagna.

Nick's lasagna.

The one he so thoughtfully made for them in Daniel's kitchen. He didn't want her to starve. Kate sniffed. It was so sweet of him.

The frozen lasagna was making Kate cry.

How she wished she could go back to those early days together. She wished he could be the awkward and adorable nerd forever. How she wished Nick had never left.

The lasagna made a clunking sound when she set it on the counter. It was frozen solid. She sniffed and carefully unwrapped it before zapping it and tossing herself a salad. One of those bag jobs; making salad for one with a whole head of lettuce seemed such a waste.

Kate sat at the granite kitchen counter and faced the small television normally hidden in the cupboard, watching the news update, munching on her salad and waiting for her lasagna to heat up.

"Hello. This is Duke Winston and we're here in L.A. with San Francisco Bay area philanthropist Nick Atwood coming up next. So stay tuned."

Kate coughed, nearly choking on her food.

Nick on Duke Winston?

Kate didn't want to see it. She wanted to turn it off and never think of him again.

He was in L.A., and here she was three hundred miles away. She didn't need to see this. She turned off the TV with the remote.

She shouldn't see it, not with her Ban Nick campaign. She was trying to get over him. Watching him on TV was *not* getting over him.

Kate had to stay strong. Strong.

She turned the TV back on and resolved to be "strong" after the show.

"We're here live in L.A. with Nick Atwood. Nick worked as a software engineer in Silicon Valley, California, is that right?"

"I'm still employed as a software engineer, Duke. And I'm just a regular, everyday guy."

"A regular guy, you say, but lately you've made a big splash and are the unofficial representative for the American Rainy Day Fund. I'm sure they're very pleased with all the publicity you've generated, not to mention the donations from some notable celebrities."

Nick smiled. Kate was probably the only one watching who knew it was a shy one.

"Everyone has been very generous. I really believe if Americans hear of others giving—local companies, national corporations, community members, celebrities, anyone in the media, it makes them want to donate as well."

Duke sat back in his chair. "Well, I don't want to be left out. So let's take care of this up front." He held up what looked to be a personal check. "No fanfare, please. I just want to do my part." He handed it to Nick, then pointed at it. "I want you to notice how many zeros there are."

"Yes, there are many zeros." Nick stared at the check and chuckled. "Thank you very much."

"Now that that's out of the way, tell me how all this came about? How did all this movement get started? Was it your idea?"

Nick had never come across nervous before, but in this interview he was different. Something had changed. Kate could sense something, a tension in his body, some kind of awkwardness.

"You don't work directly for the Rainy Day Fund, do you?"

"That's correct."

Duke encouraged Nick to tell his story and Kate didn't pay much attention. She'd heard the story many, many times and what she did watch was him—his posture, his hands, his eyes.

"What are you hoping will happen in all this? Personally, I mean. You've gotten more than the allotted fifteen minutes of publicity with the media, on television, what's next?

"I'm not looking to get anything out of this for myself. I support the Foundation and its goals. If I can bring some attention to their cause . . . I'm all for it."

"You've met a lot of influential people in the last couple weeks. I think most of them are taken by you."

"I don't know about that." There was fleeting expression, a flash of his bashful side that Kate spotted. She might be the only one who had recognized it.

"I heard that after you appeared on *Chloe*, she made a donation."

"Yes, she did."

"And after you appeared on William Brandish's show the host was coaxed into opening his checkbook as well."

"I wouldn't say he was coaxed but yes, he made a donation." Nick smiled, he couldn't look at Duke.

"What's your secret? How do you get these people to be so generous?" With a jab of his finger he said, "And they're doing it publicly."

"They're already generous people. I don't know why they do it. Why did you do it, Duke?"

Duke straightened and leaned back in his chair. "Wait a minute, *I'm* the host. *I* ask the questions." He laughed. "Getting people to open up their wallets is a real talent, I tell you." Duke punctuated with the nod of his head. "I can imagine there would be a lot of interest in you from some of the big corporations who'd like to have a guy like you working for their team. They could put your talents to good use."

"I'm not interested in keeping a high profile." Nick shook his head slowly. "I'm just a software programmer. After all this is said and done, I'm going back to coding." He paused. "There's someone"—he rubbed the corner of his eye—"who played a very important part in all this who I haven't had a chance to thank."

Did Kate see what she thought she saw? Rubbing an eye was one of the signals they'd used. Was he just "rubbing his eye" because it itched or was he *rubbing his eye* as in signaling?

Kate leaned forward, perching on the edge of her chair. Her gaze glued to the television screen, watching Nick more carefully, looking for another signal.

He did it again. The same hand, the same eye.

Nick sat back and held his hands together in front of him. Kate waited to see what he'd do next.

He was talking about her, and secretly in front of the viewing public *to* her.

"I'm an engineer and socially challenged by nature. I have to acknowledge that I needed some help with my socializing skills, and I did receive help but then events in my life sort of swept me away"—Nick rubbed the edge of his eye again—"so I guess you can say I have some unfinished business."

Nick stared into the camera lens and touched his chin with one fist, then touched his chin with the other in a deliberate, peculiar gesture. It was the one that Raymond had made up while goofing off.

"Now—wait a minute—what was that?" Duke paused, sitting up in his chair.

Nick repeated the gesture.

"What are you doing?" He pointed at Nick's hand, confusion clouding his face.

But it was perfectly clear to Kate.

That signal . . . it meant . . . Kate thought back. It meant. . . .

I love you.

Nick had hoped Kate had been watching and she got his message loud and clear. Even if she did, he didn't know what was going to happen next. He didn't know exactly how else to reach her, not unless he showed up on her doorstep tomorrow and even if he did she might not open the door.

How many times had he picked up the phone to call her? How many times had he wished she'd call him to "catch up on things," but that never happened. And he wasn't sure why.

She had never been out of his thoughts for more than a heartbeat. Maybe he'd imagined their closeness, attraction. He might have misinterpreted what he'd meant to her. After all, he wasn't the best at social interactions.

What she'd taught him had served him well. He was comfortable around people and they genuinely seemed to like him.

He didn't feel like the nerdy outcast he once was. Maybe he had her all wrong and now he'd put himself out there. Duke Winston and all of America wouldn't understand his actions, but Kate would.

If she were watching.

The real question was, did she care and would she do anything about it?

If she hadn't felt the same, she could deny she had seen the show at all. But he had to try. How else could he tell her how he felt? He'd let too much time pass, he had to do it now.

"This is Duke Winston and we're here with Nick Atwood, the most generous man in America."

Off to one side, Nick read *Los Altos, California* on the lower part of the monitor.

Duke pressed a button. "You're on the air, caller, go ahead."

Los Altos? Could it be . . . ?

"Good evening, Duke."

Nick recognized her voice. It was her. Kate.

"I was wondering, Duke . . . after Mr. Atwood is finished with his current flurry of public appearances, if he'll be heading home."

"Good point, caller." Duke turned from the camera and faced Nick. "You have a family to get back to, and sooner or later you have to return to your job so you can earn the salary which you've so generously donated. How soon will you be returning to your normal life?"

Hearing Kate's voice made Nick get all choked up. He couldn't answer immediately. During his moment's silence Duke jumped in.

"Or will you bounce from L.A. to New York?"

Duke kept the questions coming, turning the heat up. "I've heard you've made some very pretty new friends. Shall we name names?"

Nick hoped not.

"I think"—Nick could feel his voice shake and tried his best to keep it from cracking—"I will have finished my obligations after tonight and by tomorrow morning I'll be heading back to the Bay area." He stared into the camera and hoped with all his heart Kate that could read the love he held for her in his eyes. "I've missed home more than I can say."

Chapter Fifteen

It was Tuesday, 8:44 AM.

Without a word, Nick walked into Kate's office and pushed the door closed. His sudden appearance caught Kate off guard and she fumbled with the remote control before stopping the VCR. But not before he'd seen what she was watching and she felt embarrassed.

Nick walked toward her with his shoulders straight and his head held high. Quite a difference since the first time he'd walked into her office. This was not the shy awkward software engineer who'd been here a month ago.

"I've changed a lot since then, haven't I?" He nodded toward the darkened television.

"Not as much as you think." There was nothing for him to be ashamed about.

They were together. Alone. And it felt strange. It never had before. Not between them.

The dynamics had changed. No longer were they student and teacher but equals, man and woman.

"So I guess we have some unfinished business," he began and Kate still didn't know what to say.

She stared at him and realized that he looked different. The salon-styled hair and superficial cover-model good looks he had were gone, replaced by his own, redefined personal style and an air of confidence.

He had managed to take what he'd learned and blend it with the person he was and make it work for him. And it was working for him. He was as handsome, as irresistible, as ever.

His hair had a slight part on the left, and the front was brushed casually to the side. He wore thin wire-rimmed glasses, giving him a studious look. To Kate, there was nothing sexier to her than a smart man.

"The last few weeks have been . . . awful. I tried to keep in touch." Nick paused. "I didn't think I'd be away this long. I didn't think we'd ever have the time to have a simple phone call. I didn't think. . . ."

"I called you. I left you voicemails on your cell phone."

"Voicemail?" Nick sighed in defeat. "I never

thought to—I don't know how to use that phone. I never had the time to read the manual."

"I thought you were busy. Too busy." Kate pushed the words out angrily and held back her tears.

"Too busy for what? You?" Nick shook his head. "How could you think that?"

"What about . . . the other women?" It was difficult for Kate to get the words out. They were words she didn't want to say to a question she didn't want to know the answer to. But she had to ask, she had to know.

"*What* other women?"

"Those women that I hear on the phone in the background. The women, beautiful actresses. They've been calling for you. Calling the office."

Could it be true? Had Nick never noticed the Hollywood hunnies who pursued him?

Nick took her hand to keep her from moving away from him. "Aw, Kate. How can I tell you how much you mean to me?"

"But everyone loves you. Your family, the media, those Hollywood actresses. How could I ever compare to them?" Kate hadn't felt so insecure in years. Nick could probably have his pick of anyone on the planet, how could he want her?

"You don't have to compare yourself to anyone." He perched on the edge of her desk and pulled her close, wrapping his arms around her. "Did you hear me? I said I love *you*."

"What?" Kate blinked, wondering if there was something wrong with her ears.

"I love you." Nick whispered. His warm breath brushed across her neck, and he kissed her.

He wouldn't joke with her about this would he? "What about Judith Lonsdale and Guinevere Baker?"

"What about them?"

"They're beautiful; they want you." She couldn't believe how Nick's life had changed. He was a celebrity. Everyone wanted a piece of him. How could all that attention not sway him, change him? And she wondered if there'd be any left for her in the end.

"They're very nice, but I don't want them." Nick pulled a soft handkerchief from inside his jacket and wiped Kate's tears from her checks.

"How could you not want them? How could you—"

Nick covered her mouth with his and kissed her. Not only was he convincing her, he was making her feel dizzy. Her toes tingled and she wrapped her arms around him to keep from hitting the floor.

She felt so good in his arms. Kate never wanted him to let go.

"And you love me, right?" he whispered into her hair.

She did. Why was she afraid to say it?

"I thought there was something between us, or did I imagine that?" An expression of doubt crossed his face.

Nick hadn't imagined anything. There was something between them. She loved him, but could he love her?

Kate was sure there must have been others. She didn't want to make herself insane by thinking how many women were in love with Nick.

"I'm not interested in them. They don't know the real me, the me who wore a ponytail and those silly sandals. You're the only one who does." He glanced away, and Kate thought he was masking a bit of guilt. "It took me a while to realize that. I thought you might have fallen for the new and improved Nick."

He took such a chance opening up to her. Kate was in love with him, had been almost from the very beginning.

"You were watching my tape when I walked in here. Were you laughing at the way I used to be—nervous and nerdy?"

Kate sprang to his defense. "Of course you were nervous, but you had the courage to convince me to help you after I'd made up my mind I couldn't. Not at first, not until I saw how you weren't going to take no for an answer."

"That's right, you remember that. I always get what I want."

"Nick . . ." she smiled and new tears moistened her eyes.

"Why are you crying now?"

"Because I do love you."

"Is that something to cry about?"

Kate took his handkerchief and wiped her eyes. "I may have taught you how to interact and deal with the opposite sex, but you'll just have to face the fact that you'll never understand women. No man does."

"That doesn't matter as long as I have a lifetime to study you, I'm sure I'll do just fine. I'm a good student, you know."

"Yes, you are—" She stopped. "Lifetime?" Did he mean what she thought he meant? Marriage?

Raymond buzzed in on the intercom.

"Doctor O'Connor, *Stylin'* Magazine waiting on the line for Nick. They want to schedule your bachelor photo shoot."

"*Stylin'* Magazine?" Kate stared wide-eyed at Nick as he reached to answer his call, wondering what the heck could be going on.

Bachelor photo shoot?

Kate lifted the phone receiver and handed it to Nick.

"Nick Atwood here." He paused, listening for several seconds and finally said, "I understand. I'm sorry. Yes, thank you. No, I don't have a publicist anymore. I'm very flattered, but I don't think that's going to be possible."

He glanced up at Kate but spoke into the phone. "I can't be in your Fifty Most Eligible Bachelors issue because I won't be a bachelor. It's that simple. I'm sorry. Yes, I understand. Okay, fine. 'Bye."

Nick hung up the phone and smiled at Kate.

"I could call them back and tell him our wedding is off if that's what you decide."

Kate was still searching for words. The first one she came up with was, "No!"

"I'm bachelor number seven, you know." He smiled in a teasing sort of way. "They said they'll hold my spot. I can always call them back."

"Don't you dare." Kate pulled Nick to her and kissed him. She tried to kiss him as breathless as he'd kissed her, make him weak in the knees, make certain he knew no one else could love him as she did.

Nick let out an exhausted sigh when they parted. "That was some kiss. Is that a yes? Will you marry me, Kate?"

Kate snuggled into his chest and smiled. "Yes, I'll marry you." She kissed him again. "Only number seven? To me, you're number one."